I0618875

OMNICIDE

JACQUELINE DRUGA

PRESS

Published by Vulpine Press in the United Kingdom in 2020

Cover by Lindsey Thorburn at Dark Heart Designs

ISBN: 978-1-83919-331-6

www.vulpine-press.com

To my sons, Noah and Drew, for their demonstration of what it truly means to be brothers.

1.
PAVEMENT

May 7

"This is Modine, do you copy?" The deputy gave it a few seconds as he cruised down the secondary highway. He brought the microphone to his mouth again. "Calling Seaver, this is Deputy Modine from Griffin, do you copy?"

Nothing.

He shook his head, and looked up to the rearview mirror, catching a glimpse of his tired eyes. Christopher 'Kit' Modine had been going nonstop for at least twenty-four hours. He looked old; he wasn't. Around his eyes were dark circles, and the fine lines were more prominent. It was the strangest call he had been on in his twenty years of police service.

Then again, it really wasn't a call.

After one more, "This is Modine. Seaver, do you copy?" he switched radio channels. "Griffin, this is Modine."

The radio crackled and so did the transmission. It was distorted but Kit understood the male voice.

"We can barely hear you. You must be close."

No shit, that's why I'm driving out here, Kit thought to himself. Instead he just replied, "Three miles. I'll radio back when I can."

A staticky, "Be careful" came over the radio.

"Roger that, out." Before he set down the radio, he switched the station and tried one more time. "Seaver, do you copy?"

Still no reply. He had been trying steadily since he left Griffin nearly thirty miles away.

Seaver was the closest town, one Griffin regularly communicated with several times a day. But since the day before...nothing.

Kit volunteered to be the one to venture to the town too far away for a reliable radio transmission.

Just about there, he spotted a red pickup truck on the road. It wasn't moving, in fact, it was parked slanted across the road. As Kit drove closer he could see the driver's door was open.

He knew the truck.

It belonged to Hillbilly Jim. Not that Donald Smith was a hillbilly or even named Jim—it was a nickname he had gotten when he protested the changing date of the county refuse pickup. He grew his beard long and bushy and looked like the legendary wrestler Hillbilly Jim. It was strange. As if his hairy face would make the county change their mind about picking up garbage on Mondays instead of the new day, Thursday.

Kit was pretty sure it wasn't Hillbilly Jim's beard that caused them to go back to Mondays, but everyone else thought it was and Don 'Hillbilly Jim' Smith kept the beard and became a legend.

A legend whose truck was eerily abandoned a quarter mile outside of town.

Kit didn't want to admit to himself that he found the sight unnerving. The truck just left there on the outskirts of a town that had dropped all communications.

He parked right there, right by Hillbilly Jim's truck and, just in case someone could hear, he radioed home to let them know he'd arrived and that he didn't think all was well in Seaver.

Kit stepped from the squad car, leaving his door open and the car running, and he walked the ten feet to the open truck door.

No one was in there and Kit examined it closely.

The keys were still in the ignition in the 'on' position, yet the truck was dead. It had run until he'd run out of gas.

Why would Hillbilly just up and leave his truck?

The interior was the typical mess. A few empty packs of smokes, a coffee in the holder, candy wrappers.

No driver.

Kit looked toward town; he didn't see any movement and he returned to his squad car.

Typically, he would have walked, had he not had his friend's voice in the back of his head talking all kinds of end-of-the-world crap she saw in movies.

Kit didn't believe in zombies and didn't worry about them, but something was amiss in the town of Seaver and he wasn't taking any chances if he had to get away.

Like Hillbilly.

He drove the two blocks, stopped again, and opened the car door just outside of Frieda's books.

It didn't take much for him to know something was really wrong.

It was quiet, not a noise to be heard.

No one was racing in and out of the coffee shop.

Not a soul on the street.

Kit had driven all the way there. He knew he had to at least investigate.

Did the people leave? Did they evacuate for some reason?

It took only for him to step from the car to know it was something bigger than that. He heard a crunching sound the second his foot hit the pavement.

Slowly, Kit looked down.

On the ground everywhere were birds and bugs, as if every living creature had just dropped from the sky.

They decorated the streets like litter after the Fourth of July event.

Kit knew.

The people of Seaver didn't leave, he just hadn't seen them yet.

They were there. What state they were in, whether they were like the birds and bees and other insects, remained to be seen.

2.
YES, DEAR

May 4—Three Days Earlier

They argued.

Of course, that was commonplace for the young couple after any instance where they visited Brad's mother.

The hour-drive home offered them plenty of time to argue it out, and usually they were done and better by the time they made it to their two-bedroom apartment in Prescott. Having just left the small town of Griffin not even ten minutes earlier, they still had a good deal of 'hashing it out' time left.

Brad put out his cigarette in an old soda can he had tucked in the driver's side door well. He yawned once, thinking he was in the clear. After all, to him, the night went well.

Or so he thought, and he stretched to put on the radio.

"Oh, no." Jenson reached forward, stopping Brad from turning on the radio. "We talk."

"Oh my God," he said with a shake of his head. "What is there to talk about?"

"Um…the visit."

"It's always the same thing, Jen. You start with how my mother hates you…"

"She does."

"No, she doesn't."

"Then she doesn't like me," Jenson said.

"She does, too, like you. Why does it always have to start with this? Every single time?"

"Because you fail to acknowledge my feelings."

"You know, I can write the script for this," Brad said. "Save you the trouble."

"Why don't you see it?"

"What is there to see?"

"She stares at me weirdly, doesn't look me in the eye."

"My mom has that eye thing," Brad replied.

"She made ham."

"So."

"I hate ham."

"Oh my God."

"Why do you always defend her?" Jenson asked.

"She's my mom. I'm her only child."

"No, you are not."

"Okay, but I'm the favorite."

"I'll give you that."

Brad shook his head. "Is there anything new that happened tonight, aside from my mom not liking you, cooking you foods that aren't your favorite, and making fun of her lazy eye?"

"I did not."

"You did. Now give me ten minutes of radio." Brad reached down for the button.

"Can we not...deer."

"Sweetheart."

"No...deer."

Brad hit the brakes instinctively before he even looked up fully.

Jenson had good eyes. She'd spotted it making its way onto the dark road long before Brad would have.

It was ten feet in front of them, stopped.

But something was off.

Brad thought at first the six-point buck was being brazen as it made its way slowly to the car, but it was something else.

"What's wrong with it?" Jenson asked.

"I don't know."

Something was.

His hind legs weren't steady, they wobbled as if he were a newly born fawn. His head swung from left to right, not smoothly, but with jerking motions as his mouth opened in some sort of silent cry.

He moved sideways as if trying to loft his body.

What looked like a huge sore graced above his back leg, but more alarming than that was the color of his fur. It was greyish brown, almost completely gray, which was far from the reddish-brown color it should have been for July.

"Is he hurt?" Jenson asked. "I think he's hurt."

"Or sick."

"He could have been hit by a car."

"We need to call the state police," Brad said. "Let them know. He isn't moving from this road."

"I don't think he can," she said.

"Pull up the map on your phone," Brad said, watching the buck continue in its behavior. "Ping where we are so I can let them know." He grabbed his own phone.

"I feel so bad for him."

"Yeah, me too."

"We're not far. We haven't passed the Dairy Delight yet."

Brad had eyes on the deer as he blindly tried to dial the three simple numbers. It was just before he hit send that the buck violently hurled himself toward the car. Like someone trying to break down a door, he slammed side first into the front end.

Both Brad and Jenson jumped.

He slammed into the car again with an elk-sounding cry.

Brad knew the animal hadn't a clue what he was doing. He was hurt or ill and his actions were out of the control. Or maybe even the creature was trying to find some relief.

Brad tossed the phone down, threw the car in reverse and backed up. Again, it aimed for the car. Hurriedly, after putting the car in drive, Brad jerked the wheel, went around the deer, and peeled past it with spinning tires.

"Jesus," Jensen gasped out holding her chest.

"Call. They need to know."

"Maybe he's gone," Jenson suggested.

Brad looked up to the rearview mirror the same time Jenson turned to look back.

The buck was still on all fours, shaking and thrusting its body forward to nothing in a dance of pain.

Their eyes were on him. Only for a second or two.

Not on the road.

A second or two was all it took.

By the time Brad lowered his eyes from the mirror, because of the accelerated speed, their four-door sedan slammed head-on into another large buck. The animal flew up into the air, bounced on the hood and through the windshield.

The car swerved out of control. Brad couldn't see a thing past the animal that took up his entire view. Not only was it still alive, but thrashing relentlessly half in and half out of the car.

Brad's foot powered toward the brake but it was too late.

The car smashed into something, ejecting the airbags. Brad felt it hit into his face and his head banged into the driver's side window. There was nothing he could do, it was out of his control. The car tilted, rolling on two wheels before hitting another object and coming to a dead stop.

He was conscious in that brief moment after. He didn't know if he was ready to pass out or ready to die.

The buck was still in his car, more so now than before. Still alive, its grunts and huffs mixed with the sound of a car horn blasting steadily in the distance. Brad couldn't see Jenson. He tried. He couldn't turn his head, couldn't call out.

In fact, he couldn't move. He just had to sit there and wait and hope that help would arrive.

3.
SCOOP

May 5

Griffin, Arizona was a town out of time. A lot of the town's buildings looked like something from the doo-wop era. Meticulously maintained for the benefit of the small but steady tourist season that happened upon them every summer.

Griffin was isolated.

The closest town in all directions was thirty miles away. A green view from one side of town, a brown from the other, Griffin was nestled between a desert and the mountains and was smack dab on the course of the famed Route 66. The residents often said the town was the basis for the famous animated movie starring automobiles.

The story was the same.

At one time it was always busy, but with the construction of the interstate it was more of a novelty. A standing icon to an era long gone.

They paid tribute to that era by keeping up the throwback appearance, although many said the decade they most paid tribute to was the nineties. Because more times than not they were stuck with landline, dial-up speed internet when the Wi-Fi signal was lost.

Looks and technology, the town of three thousand was a throwback showcase. They still had a print edition newspaper with a staff of three. For a while they operated every day, twice on Sunday, but that dwindled down to four days a week.

They'd never really get rid of the print edition all together. They couldn't. People needed their news. When the Wi-Fi went down, so did the cable. It took too long to download the pictures on the web edition; one could make and eat a sandwich before the weather report loaded. The local TV station got their news from the *Griffin Times*.

The *Griffin Times* got theirs mainly from the AP wire.

Any way they could.

They still used a fax faithfully and Walt, the editor, had his great-grandfather's teletype machine that occasionally spouted off when Walt called the New York office to say they were down again. Headlines would auto type away sounding like a data printer. Which…*Griffin Times* still had.

Hiring practices at the *Times* were less skill based and more of a twisted nepotism. An inherited right to work there.

At least with the three employees that held down the fort. Walt Sommers was the editor-in-chief. His great-grandfather times five had started the paper, and it had been handed from one generation of Sommers to the next.

Brian's '*Griffin Times* Genealogy' dated back to his great-grandmother who was a typist. Brian was the best writer of the three. He hated that people requested him for obituaries.

The backstory of Cass was similar to Walt's, at least three generations of her family had worked at the *Times*. Most famously her father, who was best known as Scoop McDaniels. A nickname Cass had not yet lived up to. Not yet. It wasn't for lack of trying.

It wasn't to say the three of them made a living or career from working at the *Times*. Brian was a high school teacher; Walt ran the local car repair and body shop. Cass didn't need more than her part-time income. She lived quite comfortably off the inherited remaining balance of her grandfather's Publishers Clearing House sweepstakes win. He took the thousand dollar a week payoff which she now collected.

The *Griffin Times* was the glue in the center that held the town together more than people wanted to admit.

It gave it the sense of small town, keeping things real and personal.

Griffin was far removed and in a sense was like its own entity.

An alien nation.

In fact, that was what Cass called the town of Griffin in a piece she wrote about how culturally different they were than the rest of the world. How Griffinites weren't pampered but were self-reliant.

They were down to earth and as old-fashioned as they came.

The fact that they all still had and used landlines proved that.

Cass was the first one in the office, she figured she would be. Walt talked about how he had to pound out the dent on the Marshal car and Brian never got up before eight during non-school months.

In frustration, Cass set her phone on the desk. She hated that it seemed like every time a cloud rolled in they didn't get a cell signal.

What was the point of the new tower being built?

She had to use the landline.

"No," she said into the phone. "Not Cassandra. Cass. Short for Cassia." She rubbed her eyes. "It's a flower. Yes, look it up. Can you…thank you. Anything you got." She hung up the receiver of the black phone. She could smell the brewing coffee and that made her happy.

There wasn't much she could do until she either got a signal, heard the fax or the tickity-tick-tick-tick-tick of the teletype as it rang out.

She just sipped her coffee and sat at the desk when she saw Brian walk in; he was a semi-tall man, slightly on the slender side, the kind of high school teacher Cass wish she'd had when she went to Griffin High.

"Hey," she said. "You're early."

"I couldn't sleep," he replied, sitting on the edge of her desk. "I was playing video games all night, not, mind you, connected to the Wi-Fi, so I had to resort back to 1994 Nintendo and those images wouldn't leave my mind when I closed my eyes."

"I hate that. I was binge-watching *Of Men and Stone*…"

"You never watched that? It ended like three years ago."

"I know. I refused to join the craze. Last night, final season, last two episodes…bam, internet goes out. I could have finished," Cass said.

"You have to."

"Don't tell me what happens."

"I won't. Is that why you're in early?" Brian asked.

"No, I'm on literary punishment, remember. Now"—she tossed out her hand—"I'm stuck on the bug story."

"The bug story?"

"Yeah, Walt wants me to do a piece on the Monatrod…di am— something or other."

"The pred bug?" Brian asked.

"Pred bug, bully bug, whatever you call it."

"That's pretty important news."

13

"It's old news," she said. "Yeah, I mean, granted last year when they"—she held her hands up doing quotes—"popped up."

"Why did you just air quote?" he asked.

"Because I don't believe for a second they just evolved. That doesn't happen. Look, like everyone else, I hate the stinkbug. Hate them. But they served a purpose. Then again, I don't think the stinkbug just happened either."

"No, they were brought over," Brian said. "To control the pests that were wreaking havoc on the crops. Until they became the pest."

"Freaking Chinese."

"What?" Brian laughed the word. "Why are you cursing the Chinese?"

"Because they created the stinkbug and then they were a problem so they created a bug that would kill them. Now that bug is eating everything in sight, defeating the whole entire natural or unnatural purpose of creating the stinkbug in the first place."

"Well at least we created something to get rid of the pred bug."

"Yeah," Cass said. "And what's next? They'll need something to destroy that."

"I don't think so…"

"Oh!" She snapped her finger. "Maybe that's it. Maybe he wants me to do an investigative piece on how the government created the bug that almost destroyed humanity."

Again, Brian laughed. "How is that?"

"Kill the crops, starve the people."

"I don't think it's deliberate and your investigative reporter skills are what got you in trouble. Are you forgetting why Walt was pissed? You can't write a story based on your theories."

"I had proof."

"What proof did you have that the chief of police was banging his assistant?"

"In cell three."

"Cass."

"Mark's sister's best friend's cousin was in cell two sleeping it off. And it's awfully convenient that the camera wasn't working."

"No, it's not," Brian said. "Everything goes down in this town."

"Apparently so does the chief of police in cell three."

Brian shook his head. "Write the pred bug story and accept your punishment. You're just lucky your ex-husband is the mayor and got the chief to drop the libel suit."

"That's because he has something on the chief."

"Stop," Brian said with a lighthearted tone. "Work on your story."

"I can't. I'm waiting for info to come in from the AP, I'm just gonna run a repeat."

"That's cheating."

"No it's not," Cass argued.

"Just…go online."

"It's down," Cass said.

"No, it's back."

"Shit." Cass spun her chair to the computer. "Think I can catch an episode of *Of Men and Stone* before—"

"No." Walt's voice carried into the small office. He walked in wearing his car shop uniform. "I need you to cover something else. Actually, probably both of you."

"Drop the pred bug story?" Cass asked.

"Yeah, I'll grab a copy from the AP and do a rerun."

Cass gave a smug look to Brian.

"What's up?" Brian asked.

15

"Last night there was a three-car accident on Miller Run Road."

"There were three cars on Miller Run at the same time?" Cass asked. "No one is ever on that road."

"I know, I thought it was strange too. Two of the cars were tourists that got lost," Walt said.

"Any casualties?" Brian asked.

"Three casualties, four injuries."

Brian whistled. "Why do you need the story covered by us both."

"As a favor to Marge Wakefield," Walt replied. "Her boy was in the accident."

Cass gasped. "Brad? Oh my God. Is he…?"

Walt shook his head. "No, thank God. He's in the hospital. But Jenson was killed."

"Oh no," Cass said. "Poor Brad. Marge never really liked her. So she has to feel really bad, too."

"Anyhow, she seems to think you're the next Scoop McDaniels after the sex scandal story and wants you to look into it. See if something else happened up there. If, you know, Cass, you're okay with it."

Cass nodded. "Yes. Don't worry about it."

Walt continued. "Anyhow…Brad is unconscious, the others are alert and aware and she wants answers. As you can understand."

"More than you realize," Cass said.

"No, I do," Walt said. "All three cars are at our shop. State Police were there. See what you can find out and then, Cass, you write up about the accident…Brian, write a nice piece about Jenson."

"Obituary," Brian said less than enthused.

"Celebration of life stories, Brian, celebration of life," Walt replied. "We don't call them obits anymore. And I have to head back to the shop. Keep in touch. Let me know what you got. I'll edit the stories for tomorrow's edition if you can get it together."

Cass nodded her acknowledgement. Walt was solemn, which was unusual. After another swig of her coffee, Cass stood. "Ready?" she asked Brian.

"Ready…Scoop."

"That is such a compliment from Marge," Cass said, as she grabbed her purse and walked to the door. "She has faith that I can get to the truth."

"Yes, she does, but…unfortunately for you, Scoop, this isn't an investigative piece," Brian said and opened the door for her. "It's just a car accident. Nothing less, nothing more."

4.

RASH

Gyles Farm, Saline County, Nebraska

Larry Gyles swore he wouldn't be one of them, but he was. He would
have sworn, if he were hit, it would be nothing…but it wasn't.

Far from it.

As a farmer he knew his crops, he knew the normal smell of his
land that carried through his open window.

He knew when he'd woken up two days earlier that something
was amiss.

Larry wasn't much of a television guy; he barely watched it. He
did listen to the radio. Mostly, if he couldn't read the news, he didn't
know what was going on.

Fortunately, information was delivered to his house.

A flyer from the Department of Agriculture stated that extermination proceedings had begun for the pred bug, and should he, as a
farmer, experience the insect before his farm was treated he was to
call a number at the bottom of the paper.

That was a mere twenty-four hours before he was hit.

He had heard about the new breed of insect and how they were
fast moving and devastating. That they could easily cause agricultural
annihilation.

Whatever that was.

Larry had taken that as an exaggeration.

Until two days earlier, when he woke up.

A faint steady clocking sound carried to him through the quiet of the dark early morning hours. He made his coffee, got dressed, and went to the barn to work on the tractor. While in there, he heard Leo's truck pull up. Leo was his head farmhand and had been with Larry for twenty years.

It wasn't long after that Leo, in a panic, flung open the barn door.

"Larry, we have problems. Big problems," Leo said.

Larry put down the wrench, wiped his hand, and walked toward the door.

The sun had started to rise, giving light to the sky. Larry expected to walk out and have to follow Leo somewhere. But that wasn't the case.

When he'd left his home earlier that morning, it was still dark. He didn't see.

Now it was light, he did.

Larry didn't have to go far, not even twenty feet outside the barn and he could see, actually as far as he could see, his corn, which the day before had been green and flourishing, was gone.

Completely gone.

Suppressing his initial panic and anger, Larry took a closer look.

If he were to venture a guess, Larry would say there were millions. And that wasn't an exaggeration. Millions of those pred bugs everywhere.

Nothing shook them.

They were a new breed of bugs eating everything they could.

They alone eradicated the stinkbug then moved on, evolving.

The bugs, over the course of the past year, had become stronger, more brazen, and impervious to anything used to kill insects before.

Every use of known insect pathogenic bacteria had failed.

Until a new pathogen was created. Awfully fast, many thought. But it was there and it worked.

It was successful and killed the pred bugs so quickly there wouldn't be time for them to build an immunity. It was being called the five-day Bug Blitzkrieg. It was the government's hope that any pred bug not killed right away would carry the new pathogen, spreading it like a plague among them. Eventually eliminating the need for the government to disperse the germ.

Larry placed the call.

He was told that while the pathogen wasn't harmful to humans, to be safe he and his staff had to stay indoors while the pred bugs were sprayed.

Two hours later a plane arrived. That wasn't before Larry estimated he had lost at least twenty acres of crops.

He, Leo, and four other workers watched from his living-room window. They waited the hour as instructed and then they went out.

The six of them sought out the heavy equipment—they had the acreage to clear. Plowing it, removing what was left of the crops and the bugs.

A click here and there was heard, but for the most part, Larry knew they were dead.

The second he took his first step into the field he heard the crunching under his shoes and the comments from Leo and the other workers.

"It snowed bugs," Leo said. "Lar, this is going to take us forever to get through. What exactly do we do with them?"

"Burn them," Larry replied.

By the time an early lunch break rolled around, they had cleared a measly third. To Larry it was disheartening. Usually he would keep going, but this time, he welcomed the break and went back to his house to wash up.

He removed his face mask and gloves and even used his elbow to turn on the kitchen sink. Once his hands were wet he grabbed the soap and started to scrub.

Fingers, hands, elbows...stop.

No sooner did the soap cross the bend of his elbow, he felt a stinging pain, as if he had rubbed against a brush burn.

He flipped on the cooler water and rinsed, then grabbed a towel. He dried off, still feeling the sting, then twisted his arm until he was able to see.

Just below the elbow on the back of his forearm was a large, deep red mark. An area the size of a lemon was bright and inflamed. The surface of it had a dry, yet waxy appearance.

Grunting, Larry passed it off as an allergic reaction to the pathogen used to kill the bugs, thought no more about it, and proceeded to make his lunch.

5.
GLIDED STOP

Twelve hours after an accident, Cass sort of figured there'd be nothing left there. A few shards of glass, a piece of a broken turn signal, a messed-up tree, and an awful lot of blood on the road.

Three people had died, four injured.

The state police, reportedly, were on scene, but Cass didn't understand why Griffin Police weren't…or maybe they were.

The only way to find out would be to ask.

That would warrant a trip back into town and to the station before heading to the hospital. Cass wanted some information on hand to give Marge. Something other than there was an accident. Last Cass heard that was all they'd told her.

Nothing more.

A ding-ding alert bell rang when Cass and Brian entered the Griffin police station. It always annoyed Cass. An old-fashioned bell hanging on a string—couldn't they move with the times?

Like the town, the entire police station seemed to pay homage to an era gone by. An old-style, albeit empty, sergeant's desk was directly out front, behind it a three-foot-high wooden wall to separate the front from the back. A couple of desks, a back office, and three jail cells that could clearly be seen from anywhere in the room.

"You're not supposed to be here," a voice called from the distance, then a second later Kit walked from the rear office. "You know that, right?"

"Not really. I mean I do know it, but it doesn't apply to today." Cass pushed on the Andy Griffith style waist-high swinging wood opening to walk into the main portion of the old-fashioned station. "Is he here?"

"No," Kit answered.

"Then I'm okay. I just can't be here while the chief is here. Notice I didn't say anything about Pam."

"She doesn't work here anymore," Kit replied. "She quit after your little scandal piece or I'm sure they'd have a restraining order in her name too."

"They do," said Brian. "She moved to Seaver so it's easy for Cass to avoid them."

"What's easy is the fact that she lucked out," Kit said. "That her fourth or fifth ex-husband is mayor…"

"Second," Cass corrected. "Mark is my second ex-husband."

"Second. Thank you," Kit said. "You could have been sued for libel."

"It's only libel if it's not true," Cass said. "Mark got him to see reason."

Kit waved out his hand. "And the judge made you see a thousand-foot restraining order."

"Judge Moss said a hundred feet," Cass replied. "Won't the festival be a fun place to stay a hundred feet from him."

"Speaking of which," Brian added, "they already shut down Fourth, you know. As an officer of the law you need to do something about that."

"Like what? They're setting up. The festival is tomorrow."

"Fourth isn't supposed to be shut down at all."

Kit shook his head. "Who cares. What do you guys want?'

"So nasty," Cass said, pulling out a chair. "You're usually much more cheerful." She sat down, then so did Brian.

"Oh, we're sitting?" Kit asked. "This has to be good if you're making me sit."

"Like you don't sit all day, in the car, in the office," Cass snipped.

"Cass. What?"

"The accident on Miller Run last night," Cass said.

"What about it?" Kit asked. "If you're trying to run a story, really it's basic. No drinking and driving. Just a freak accident."

"Kit," Cass said. "It was on Miller. The fact alone that there were three cars at the same time on Miller is freakish."

"Well, two of the cars were traveling together. Sort of a reunion of a Route 66 tour they do every ten years."

Brian looked curiously at Cass, then to Kit. "If they do it every ten years how were they lost and using Miller? That's what we heard."

"They weren't lost," Kit replied. "They took Miller Run on purpose to avoid Griffin.'

Cass scoffed a laugh. "Seriously? They wanted to avoid our town. Why?"

"Avoid Crazy Ada," Kit replied. "She shot at them for getting too close to her property and they won't come back."

"When?" Cass asked.

"Thirty years ago," Kit answered.

"Way to hold a grudge," Cass said. "The accident. Were you there afterward?"

Kit folded his hands on his lap as he reclined. "Yeah, yeah, I was. It was pretty bad. You know, the cars are all down at Eb's." Kit pointed back as if he were actually pointing at the garage. "If you wanna take a look. I mean, I'm sure they won't have a problem showing you, considering one owner is your editor and the other is your first ex-husband."

"Original. Never called him an ex," Cass said. "It won't be necessary right now. Marge's boy was in that. Which is why we're here. She wants answers."

"Not many to give," Kit replied. "It was an accident. Messy but an accident. His girl was killed by way of…" He raised his eyebrows a few times. "Antler."

"Antler?" Cass asked. "What do you mean antler?"

"Four- or six-point buck." Kit shrugged. "All points impaled her somewhere when the buck came through the windshield."

"Do you have pictures?" Brian asked.

"Brian," Cass scolded.

"What?" Brian lifted his hand. "It would be interesting to see."

"I have pictures," Kit said. "But like I originally said: a freak accident. Nearest we can figure, Brad hit a deer, was driving blind, the white Chevy hit a deer and—"

"Wait," Cass halted him. "Two cars, hit two deer…?"

"And Brad hit the other car."

"Two deer up on Miller Run?" Cass asked.

"Cass, it's not abnormal when they're running to find safety. Ada was up there hunting earlier in the day."

"It's not hunting season," Cass said.

"It's Crazy Ada," Kit replied. "But…" He reached into the drawer. "If you want to give Marge answers"—he pulled out a plastic bag containing a broken dash camera—"this was from one of the cars. Found it on the road. The memory card is in there. Maybe watch it. But bring that back please."

"Absolutely." Cass took it. "Thank you, Kit. And thank you for the information." She stood up and turned to leave.

"Oh, Cass." Kit snapped his finger. "I did think of something weird. The deer...they were gray-brown."

Cas tilted her head staring at him with questionable surprise.

"What?" Brian asked, confused. "What does that mean?"

"That's a winter color for them," Cass answered. "That's just really weird."

"Maybe they're sick," Brian suggested.

Kit shrugged. "If you ask Crazy Ada she says they're poisoned."

"Poisoned?" Cass questioned. "Why does she say that?"

"I don't know," Kit replied. "She was up there hunting and wouldn't shoot them because they're poisoned. Her words, not mine."

"Thanks. And..." Cass showed him the bag. "I'll bring this right back."

She and Brian walked from the station, causing the bell to ding on their exit. Once outside, Cass stopped.

"Could that mean something?" Brian asked.

"It...it could. I mean, if the deer are sick, it could have them behaving erratically. Which would give some answers to Marge. I mean, when a person you love is in an accident, you want answers. You...you need answers, you search for something to make sense of it, anything..." Cass' words trailed and her eyes seemed to drift off.

"Cass."

She jumped a little, blinking a couple times. "Yep."

"Sorry."

"No." She shook her head. "No. I'm good. Let's get back to the paper and watch the dash cam. Because I'm pretty sure we'll see all we need to on this." She lifted the camera. "If not, there's always a visit to Crazy Ada."

"That's not even funny."

"Yeah, it is. I love when you talk to her. You get all nervous."

"She's always holding a gun and aiming it at me.

"You'll have that." Cass started to walk.

"No, Cass you won't."

Cass ignored him and kept walking back to the office. She laughed a little at Brian but, she knew, once she looked at the footage, laughing would be the last thing she'd want to do.

<><><><>

Crazy Ada wasn't really crazy. Not at all. It was only those who didn't know her who called her that. And those who just got used to saying Crazy Ada. Even she referred to herself as that name when ordering pizza. It was the surefire way that the order would always be right.

Those who knew Ada knew her to be a bit eccentric and a whole lot of quirky, but they also knew her as smart, witty, and resourceful. She had the only house and piece of land considered part of Griffin but located a mile out of the town down a country road off Route 66.

She and her husband got the house with the GI loan when they were first married. They prided themselves on making their land a place to be self-reliant. Having been lifelong Griffin residents, they knew how isolated and spotty things got with technology even before the internet.

She and her husband were savvy. Both had been in the Marines for ten years. They got married and then got the house. Ada worked at the hospital as a nurse for a little while, but travel to Flagstaff was a lot when Tommy fell ill not even ten years into their marriage.

He needed constant care, and after he passed she supported herself as a firearms instructor.

Now she was more of a consultant.

Ada thought back to those early days of her really wild side when she went into town for a paper. She'd heard about the accident with the couples that avoided Griffin. Ada remembered them well and how they tried to press charges. To her it was funny because the three decades had made the incident somewhat of an urban legend. Young people told the story of how they were lost and were trying to get directions and Ada chased them with a shotgun, shooting at them the whole way.

In fact, the couple told the same story, probably even believing that was the truth after all the years of lying.

It wasn't.

Just like she told the chief of police back then, they were drunk, one tried to 'pop a squat' by her fence, and she scared them off. She never fired at them. The chief knew damn well if she did aim at them, she would have hit them. Ada didn't miss.

She heard about the tragic accident, not from the news—they didn't put out papers often enough to be up to date—but from Dale at the corner market. He told her they were up on Miller Run and Ada knew exactly what caused the accident.

The deer. They were erratic and sick for some reason. Behaving out of the ordinary. Deer in the area was uncommon. Ada heard they were there and she wanted to take advantage of it, until she saw them.

Then she changed her mind.

She told the hot cop about it, the deer and how they were sick, and he dismissed her.

Ada wanted to go back after she got her groceries and ask that cop, Kit or Cat, whatever his name was, what caused the accident, but he wasn't in. Not according to Dale the grocery clerk. The only one in was the perverted chief of police, and Ada avoided him since she heard he was a sex maniac, arresting people to have his way.

"Shame about Marge's boy," Dale said as he rung up the groceries.

"Thought you said he was just injured," Ada replied. "Not that it isn't a shame."

"His girl was killed."

"Aw, that is a shame. Marge never did like her."

"Nope." Dale shook his head. "Bet Marge is feeling guilty. I heard she has Cass on it. Might be more to what happened than meets the eye."

"Walt put Cass on the accident story. Wow."

"Yeah, go figure. My thoughts exactly."

Ada shook her head. "If you see Cass, have her come see me. I think I have an idea." After seeing the total cost, Ada pulled out her debit card and inserted it in the machine,

"Nope," Dale said. "We're down. Cards aren't working. Cash or come back."

"Damn it." She withdrew her card and lifted her bags. "I'll come back."

Dale wrote down her name.

After bidding him a farewell, she left the store. It was all too commonplace for the card machine to go down. It was the only store, probably in the country, that gave groceries on trust. As she left, Ada actually believed that the world around them could shut down and end and Griffin would probably never notice.

<><><><>

There was something sad and eerie about the footage when Cass and Brian realized it was the memory card from Brad's dash cam.

They couldn't see them, only hear them, but Brian more than Cass recognized the voices.

"Aw, man, the post in-law dinner car conversation," Brian said.

"What?" Cass asked with a laugh. "What are you talking about?"

"Okay, it's not when you leave the wife's family, just when you leave the husband's. It's a conversation about how bad it went."

"I never had that," Cass said.

"Maybe yours was a post in-law walk since you both lived in Griffin."

"Neither time. I loved my in-laws."

"That sucks."

Cass smiled and shook her head. She moved the video forward. "Just them talking. It has to happen soon."

"You know, I can write the script for this," Brad said. "Save you the trouble."

"Why don't you see it?"

"What is there to see?" he asked.

"She stares at me weirdly, doesn't look me in the eye."

"My mom has that eye thing," Brad replied.

Brian cringed. "She isn't winning this one picking on his mom."

"That's true. How does she not know about Marge and that eye thing?"

"No wonder Marge never liked her. But still, she's dead, we shouldn't talk ill of her."

"No, we shouldn't. She was still someone's child."

Brian looked solemnly at Cass. "Yeah, she is."

30

The conversation continued, they spoke about ham and other things, and Jenson kept digging a deeper hole.

"Is there anything new that happened tonight, aside from my mom not liking you, cooking you foods that aren't your favorite, and making fun of her lazy eye?"

"I did not."

"You did. Now give me ten minutes of radio," Brad said.

"Can we not...deer."

"Sweetheart."

"No, deer."

"There." Brian pointed. "Stop."

Cass did.

"Whoa," Brian said, finger aiming at the deer in the screenshot. "I'm not a deer expert but that animal looks sick to me."

"Look at the sore," Cass said. "Like it was eating itself."

"Zombie deer?'

"What? No," Cass said. "They rub up against a tree to scratch an itch. I mean, maybe he did that."

"But they didn't hit it. They stopped. I thought Kit said they hit a deer."

"He did." Cass started the video. She leaned back in her chair, watching the strange behavior of the animal.

"Yeah, there's something wrong with it," Brian repeated the sentiments playing on the recording. "I just don't..."

Cass jumped, pushing back when she saw the deer charge. "What the hell?"

"Still, they aren't moving. How did the accident happen?"

"I don't know. Leave, go around it," Cass yelled at the screen. "Don't just...okay...where...they're going..." Cass screamed. The vision of the second deer frightened her as if she were watching a horror film and something jumped out.

31

In a sense it was a horror film. For a second, they saw the accident, then the camera moved and went black. Another second or two of noise, then nothing.

Her hand went to her mouth.

"Fuck," Brian said. "I think I heard three bangs. Not sure. I can't figure out if the other car hit the crazy deer." He reached around Cass for the computer.

"What are you doing? I don't want to see the crash again."

"Not the crash…" Brian dragged the cursor then stopped. "The buck they hit." He indicated to the screen. "Same. Look. What the hell happened on that road?"

"Another sick deer." Cass stood up.

"Where are you going?"

"We need to know what happened, right? Well, the cars are all at Eb's," Cass said. "If anyone can piece together what happened by looking at the wreckage, he can."

"That's a good idea. I can't go right now, I'm meeting my wife for lunch and—"

"No, it's fine. I'm good. I'll let you know what he says." Cass grabbed her purse.

"Oh, wait," Brian called her. "Here"—he handed her the camera—"drop this off to Kit."

"I will." She took it and stopped walking. "And I think, I think I may stop by and see Ada about the deer."

"You think she's right? You think they're poisoned?"

"I don't know," Cass said. "It's something. I've hunted my entire life and never saw a deer look like that."

"So you think it's important?"

"I do. And if my gut is right, I think we may have more than a car accident story as well."

"You are the next Scoop McDaniels."

Cass smiled, gave a thumbs-up, and left the office. She didn't realize how right her gut actually was.

<><><><>

Lena Feeny loved her lip gloss. In fact she loved it so much, she had her own brand. She never went anywhere without her case full of various colors.

She undid the cap to Ruby Rose Number 3, pulled out the stem applicator, and placed it on her lips, exhaling in relief as if she had just taken a hit of some sort of drug.

"Oh my god," she said in ecstasy, closing her eyes, pursing her lips then smacking them together. It felt so good. She hadn't worn any makeup all day. That was part of her reality show. It was to be 'down home and back to basics.' Former supermodel Lena Feeny shucks her Hollywood fancy lifestyle to return to her country bumpkin roots. Something Lena never really had. A total exaggeration. A façade the public bought when Lena's *Dig It Homestyle Cooking* cookbook was a bestseller.

Lena did cook. Rather well. But she didn't learn it from living in a small town on a farm—her parents' housekeeper taught her.

The show was about her traveling across the country, stopping at small towns, eating the local favorite foods, and socializing with the people. All of it called for a non-glamorous look and makeup-free face.

Lena hated it.

She felt more naked without makeup than when she was actually naked.

Since no one would see her, she applied a little more to her face. She was certain she wouldn't be on camera.

The camera crew had gone ahead to meet them in Nevada and never realized her mini tour bus had broken down on the old highway. They'd decided they weren't stopping at Griffin, especially after Lena heard rumors about some gun-toting woman and a sex-crazed chief of police.

They were planning to breeze right through. At least the camera crew did. Just before the small town, Lena's bus broke down. The phones didn't work so the driver had walked for help.

That was two hours ago.

Lena was sure he was dead or something.

The last she heard from him was a weird text. She tried several times but the messages went unanswered. Reiterating her fear that he was dead.

The cell service was spotty so she was shocked when her video messaging rang.

"John!" she gushed upon seeing her husband's name. She answered it. "John!"

"Hey, sweetie." He was handsome, an actor with a beaming smiling face. They were without a doubt the most beautiful Hollywood couple. "Wait. Why are you wearing makeup?"

"Oh, John, the most horrible thing happened."

"What?'

"This thing I am riding in."

"The short bus"

"It broke down."

"Oh no," John said. "Where?'

"Right outside that horrid little town we were going to avoid. It's there, John, a mile up ahead."

"At least you're close to help."

"The driver left two hours ago to get help. The phones keeping going in and out. I'm alone, John. Alone on the side of the road."

"Where is the camera crew bus?" he asked.

"They went ahead."

"You wouldn't have this problem if you rode in the same bus."

"I can't do that," Lena said. "That means sharing a bathroom. No."

"Are you okay?" John asked

"No, it's hot in here."

"Step outside."

"Oh my God! I can't do that. Look." She aimed the phone.

"What am I looking at?"

"We broke down right in front of someone's property. See the house in the distance."

"Oh, yeah. Go knock on the door."

"What!" she blasted and turned the phone back around. "They're probably wearing masks made of skin. In fact, my driver is probably in the basement of that house chained up, ready to be someone's lunch."

"Lena…"

"And they're eyeing me for dinner. You know I have that extra ten pounds."

John laughed. "Lena…"

"Or worse, it could be that sex-craved chief of police's house."

"I'm sure it's fine, Lena. Really."

A triple loud rapping on the door caused Lena to jump and shriek.

"What? What is it?" John asked.

"Someone's banging on the door."

"Is it the driver? Did you lock him out?"

"Yes, but no, he has the keys. I think. Let me look." Lena peered against the window and gasped. "Oh my God there's a woman out there. She looks like my Aunt Macy. John, she has this fantastic shade of auburn hair. I'm sure it's natural, but she has an awful cut. One of those short but not short and poufy…"

"Lena, stop."

"John, she has a big gun! John, it's the gun lady."

The three knocks rang out again. And then she yelled, "I know you're in there. I see you looking out. Open the door, please."

"She's knocking again. What do I do?"

"I just heard her say open the door, please," John replied. "I'm pretty sure if she was going to shoot you, she wouldn't knock or say please."

"I can't even call the police because the chief will want to have his way with me."

"Lena, enough, open the damn door and see what she wants."

"Stay on the line?" she asked.

"Yes, I will stay…"

Beep-beep-beep rang out followed by a message on the phone that the call was lost.

Lena wanted to cry. She was scared, but she had faith in what John said about the woman probably not wanting to kill her.

Nervous, she crept toward the door, pausing to take a shot of whiskey, then before opening it, she called out, "Please don't shoot me."

"Why would I shoot you?" the woman asked.

"You have a gun."

"I always have a gun. It's my right."

"In public?" Lena asked.

"Actually it's my property so technically I'm not in public."

"I'm not trespassing," Lena told her.

"Why in God's name are we having this conversation through the door? Open up. I thought you knew I was coming."

"How would I know that?" Lena asked.

"Scott sent you a text. I was there. You replied with okay."

"Who is Scott?"

"Your bus driver."

Lena gasped and opened the door. "I'm so sorry."

"That's alright, he gave the heads-up." She walked past Lena and up the steps. "It's really hot in here. Boy this is decked out. I never saw a short tour bus."

"I like it. It's broke."

"I know."

"You said my driver texted me you were coming?" Lena grabbed her phone and read. "He didn't say. All he said was 'Ada is coming for you. I'm out.'"

"Yep." Ada smiled smugly. "That's me. I'm Ada."

"Oh!" She sang the word in revelation. "I thought he meant something else."

"Like?" Ada asked.

"I thought he mean the American Disabilities Act people were coming for me. You know because of Sam's limp."

"Who is Sam?"

"My bus driver."

"His name is Scott."

"Yes." Lena nodded. "And I bet you get that a lot. The American Disabilities Act."

"It happens," Ada said.

"Where is my driver?"

"He left," Ada said. "Hitched a ride with a couple that were finishing their meal at the diner."

"That's not very safe. Don't you have a mechanic in town?"

"We have the best."

"So why would he leave town?" Lena asked.

"Honey, he said he was out, that means…" Ada paused.

"What?"

"Probably out of money and had to go to another town to get more," Ada said. "Our ATMs only accept local debit."

"Aw, I see, well, he should have told me. I have credit cards. So are you going to help me?"

"I am. I am gonna take you into town. Walt is coming out to tow this and we can figure out what to do with you from there."

"Sounds perfect. How long will it take him to do a repair, since he's the best."

"It depends what's wrong with it," Ada replied. "Could be a few hours or a few days. Don't worry. You won't be stranded."

"Should I get my things?" Lena asked.

"You can leave stuff on here. Maybe take your purse and anything that can break during the tow."

Lena nodded once and gave a thumbs-up. She scurried for her purse, her lip gloss case, and on her away back to Ada, grabbed the bottle of whiskey.

"That works," Ada said and held the bus door opened for her.

"Ada, you don't think the police chief will try to do something with me? I heard the rumors about him."

"Only if you get arrested."

Lena was sure that wouldn't happen. Even though she had never been in trouble in her life, the rumors about the police chief were enough to make anyone into a law-abiding citizen in Griffin.

The woman Ada seemed nice, even if she carried that big gun.

Lena would make the best of the situation, break out her phone and video some footage of the town. Make the best of the time she was there. Hopefully, it wouldn't be for too long.

6.
WINGED

Even though it had been eight years, every once in a while Cass would flash back to that day.

Or rather the details of that day; the events never left her mind.

It was the taillight of one of the cars in the parking lot of Eb's shop that started it. One of the three cars involved in the accident story she as working on.

Her fingers reached down to it, running across the back end of the car, the taillights not even broken.

How was that possible when the entire front end was missing? Some things were never explainable.

Laughter.

Cass thought of how hard she and Eb laughed at the beginning of that day.

"Fifty-seven," Eb said as they drove. "Whoa. Wait. Fifty-nine."

"He's creeping up to the speed limit." Cass laughed.

"Your father will never drive the speed limit. Ever."

"I don't know what changed," Cass said. "I remember my mother always yelling at him to slow down."

"He probably never sped," Eb told her. "Just not your dad. Your mom is probably still telling him to slow down."

"We should have been the lead car," Cass said.

"No, then we'd be doing that thing where we pull over every twenty miles to wait for them."

"We may get to the Grand Canyon this week, right?" Cass joked.

Eb laughed. "Oh, wait, he's picking up speed. No, he changed his mind. Fifty-six...shit."

Truck.

"Cass?"

Eb's voice startled her some, causing her heart to skip a beat, her body to jump and a buzz in her ears. She spun around.

Withdrawing from the memory, she smiled. "Oh, hey, Eb."

"Oh, hey, Cass. I know that look on your face."

"Yep. You do." She folded her arms to her body and smiled up at him.

Eb had aged and did so well. But to her, he still looked the same as he did when they were teenagers. Tall and lanky, tattooed arms defined from working on the cars and trucks. His age was masked behind his beard with dark wavy hair that sported a wiry gray here and there.

"So," Eb said, "word on the street is you're doing the accident story."

"Considering this town has about a dozen streets it's easy to hear."

"Kit told me you were coming."

"I can't stand him," Cass said. "He's such a hotshot. He walks and struts looking like he should be doing strip-a-grams somewhere instead of enforcing the law."

"You're funny."

"He told me I wasn't allowed in the station."

"You're not."

Cass waved her finger. "Only if the chief is there. And he threw up how Mark saved my butt on that one."

41

"That's true."

"No, Mark told the chief a libel suit would only hold if it was proven false. It wasn't. So anyhow, tales of the kinky police department and my brief second husband are not why I'm here."

"The crash."

Cass nodded. "Marge thinks something was up."

"It was an accident, Cass, you know they happen."

"I do. But she wants answers. You know, how it happened. Just to understand. You have that talent."

Eb laughed. "What talent?"

"Remember when we were kids and you used to be able to look at a dent in a car and say exactly how it happened."

"Cass, if you're wanting me to say how this happened, it's pretty easy. No brainer. Don't need to be a body shop worker, insurance adjuster, or crash investigator. Any Joe or Harry can see. Three cars. Blue, driven by Brad. Gray and red driven by tourists. Gray and red cars were traveling south. They weren't moving. Both were stopped in the middle of the road, one right behind the other. Brad was going about sixty, and for some reason he just veered left, off his side, drifting into…"

Drifting.

Cass was back in the car with Eb eight years earlier, she saw that truck. It wasn't a tractor-trailer, it was a pickup truck. A newer one and bigger than normal. It was flying, and drifted into their lane…

"Cass, you listening?"

"Yeah, I'm sorry, I was just trying to picture it. Go on," she said.

"Anyhow, once Brad hit the deer he plowed into the gray car, the red car tried to move, but Brad didn't slow down, hit that too, then continued aiming left until he hit a tree."

Cass just stared.

"What?"

"That's a lot of details for anyone to figure out. I know why he drifted into the southbound lane. We watched the dashcam footage. He was too worried about the deer that was behind him."

"Another deer?" Eb asked. "I know I figured the gray car stopped for the deer that Brad hit."

"I saw the deer he didn't hit. It was winter color. You don't by chance have the one that Brad hit, do you?"

Eb chuckled. "No. But…chunks in the front end mean it was the same winter color."

"Crazy Ada told Kit that she stopped hunting yesterday because the deer are sick. I was gonna head over to talk to her. I think she's right," Cass said. "By that footage, the buck was not behaving normally."

"She may be right. I've smelled deer guts and I ain't never smelled anything this foul."

"Seriously?"

Eb nodded. "You gonna make this story about sick deer?"

"Heck yeah, if it's true, they caused the accident."

Eb's attention turned to the road. "Speaking of Crazy Ada. Walt had to tow a vehicle from her property. Broke down. You may like it."

Cass turned and looked. "Oh, wow, that's Lena Feeny's reality show bus. Is she in town?"

"I think she's at Crazy Ada's. She's not with Walt."

"Sweet. I'll talk to you later and thanks for your help." She tip-toed up and kissed him on the cheek. "Maybe I'll get an interview."

"Go get 'em, Scoop."

That made her smile. She looked back one more time to Eb, then headed to Ada's.

<><><><>

Ada had never really thought of her home as charming until Lena enthusiastically complimented it. And Ada believed her; she wasn't being polite, she was genuine.

"Oh, Ada," Lena said as they stepped into the kitchen. "Thank you for the tour. This is just rustic and charming. This kitchen is so big. It's a dream."

"Thank you."

"I take it you cook a lot."

"Nope," Ada replied. "Not at all. Not much of a cook."

"Really? This is a cook's dream kitchen."

"My husband was the cook. He designed this house. He passed and the kitchen doesn't get the use it should."

"I'm sorry about your husband."

"We had plans, you know," Ada said, "him and I. We were going to make this into a bed and breakfast one day. Everything you eat is off the land, the food, meat, water."

"Why don't you still do it?" Lena asked.

"It's a lot of work. Maybe if I had someone to help. Plus, you know"—Ada winked—"there's that bit about breakfast. I don't cook."

Lena smiled. "Now, I noticed the bedrooms were all made up. Do you have children, roommates?"

Ada shook her head. "Nope, I live alone. My niece and her kids come by to stay once a month. So I keep the rooms ready."

"This is just awesome, and your garden is equally impressive."

"Thank you. All part of the plan."

"How about pred bugs?" Lena asked. "I didn't see any signs of them."

"I have been fortunate. There haven't been any here in Griffin at all. Next town over, they got them—I think they get sprayed today. We're not getting sprayed. None of us reported them."

"Huh." Lena made the noise in surprise. "My garden in Los Angeles was ruined. Why do you suppose that is?"

"We don't have any stinkbugs…never did," Ada answered. "Stinkbugs were brought to destroy ladybugs and beetles that were killing crops. We aren't a big farm community, just gardens and years and years ago when the beetles were a problem, one of our local elders swore by his concoction. Everyone used it and that kept them away."

"What was the concoction?" Lena asked. "I mean, maybe I can share it with my viewers."

"Simple. Garlic juice and vinegar. Combine them. Keeps them all away."

Lena laughed. "Wouldn't keep me away. I love garlic and vinegar."

The doorbell drew both of their attention.

Ada stepped away toward the living room and hollered, "Come in!"

"Oh, stranger danger," Lena said. "Should you do that?"

Ada patted her sidearm. "Sweetie, I am the best shot in the county. Plus it's Griffin."

"Hey, Ada," Cass called from the other room.

"In the kitchen."

Cass entered. "Hey, Ada. Glad you're home."

"Hi, Cass. Wasn't planning on it," Ada said. "Oh, this is—"

Cass extended her hand. "Lena Feeny. I recognized your face. Plus, your truck was towed to the shop and I was there."

"Cass here is our town reporter," Ada said. "Her father was the best around and she runs a tight second. She broke the sex scandal story."

"Good for you," Lena said. "Do you cook?"

"Yeah, are you hungry?" Cass asked. "I know Ada doesn't really cook."

"Exactly," said Lena. "Did you know she has always wanted to open a bed and breakfast. But needs the help."

"Oh, stop," Ada said. "It's a pipe dream."

"You want to do that?" Cass asked. "I'll help if you want help. That sounds fun. What else do I have to do?"

"Your job," Ada said.

"Please." Cass tossed out her hand. "Plus, Walt really doesn't pay me since my inheritance." She looked at Lena. "I inherited my grandfather's Publishers Clearing House sweepstakes."

"Someone really won that?" Lena asked. "I didn't think anyone did."

"My pap. Anyhow, Ada, I'm helping Marge out with understanding what happened with the accident last night."

"Yeah, I heard you were working on that story."

"I was talking to Kit…"

"The hot cop."

Cass nodded. "He said you were trying to hunt but decided against it because the deer were sick."

"Looked it to me," said Ada. "I didn't want to take a chance."

"Take a look at this." Cass pulled out her phone. "Kit gave us the dash cam footage." She showed her the video. Lena joined in.

"Yep," Ada said. "Look at the color. It's gray.'

"It's a zombie deer," Lena said. "Look at the back leg." She jumped when she watched the deer attack.

"Aggressive," Ada said. "They weren't that aggressive when I was up there, nor did they have that sore. Could be a different buck. But I don't think so."

"Well it's not a zombie," Cass said to Lena. "And that hind leg. Caused by trying to scratch an itch. But he's tearing himself up."

"Or…" Ada said. "Something is tearing into it. Like bacteria."

"Flesh eating," Lena said. "Have here been animal cases of that?"

Ada shook her head. "A while back a dog in Wyoming had necrotizing fasciitis. But it's pretty rare. Something is foul here."

Cass snapped her finger. "Foul. Oh! Eb says he has some flesh from the buck and said it stinks worse than anything he ever smelled. Feel like taking a walk down? Give it a whiff. See what you think?"

Ada shrugged. "Sure, why not. We have to check on her bus anyhow. We can go now. Ready, Lena?"

"Without a doubt. This is exciting," said Lena. "I'm not sure I want to smell the rotting flesh, but this town sounds really interesting."

"We're boring. Zombie deer aside," Cass said. "Nothing ever happens in Griffin."

Gyles Farm, Saline County, Nebraska

Did he not wait long enough? Larry believed he knew and followed the instructions from the government about what to do after they sprayed. He waited the timeframe. Sure, the instructions stated that a small percentage of people experienced side effects, who would have known or thought Larry and his men would have hit the jackpot. They went out safely like they thought, waiting that hour as instructed. But almost immediately some of his men started getting sick. Headaches, nausea, burning skin. Larry thought maybe it was

47

psychosomatic. That was until he went inside, started to wash up and noticed the irritation on his arm. An irritation that spread quickly. Were they out there too soon? Were they too close? After all they were in the thick of the dead bugs, the chemical still latent on them.

Within half an hour of washing, Larry didn't have a headache, he didn't have nausea, but his eyes and nose burned as if he were suffering from allergies on steroids.

Thinking some rest would do the trick, he kicked off his boots, cranked up the air conditioning, downed an iced tea, and took an antihistamine. He kicked back in his easy chair and passed out.

He woke up nearly screaming. The pain in his arms was unbearable. It wasn't the burning sensation of a rash, it was a pain, a deep ache that slammed against his nerve endings, igniting them, making him feel like every bone in his arms was shattered.

He looked at the time and saw that it was still early enough to get to the urgent care in town. Without a doubt he was having some sort of severe allergic reaction. Surely, those doctors in that little place had some sort of anti-allergic reaction shot they could give him. Make it go away rather quickly. Larry was a strong man. Not much ever got him down. But the pain in his arms was kicking his butt.

It never even crossed his mind to go to a hospital until he was nearly in town. And the pain spread from his arms to his chest and to his gut. He couldn't take a breath through his nose without feeling as if it were on fire, and he passed the town and went towards Crete, a town with a university hospital fifteen miles out. He would make it. But not before his legs shook out of control, and he lost the ability to move his hands. He drove his truck using his wrists. Three or four ambulances passed him on the way there; he figured there was an accident somewhere. He never expected what he saw when he pulled up. The small hospital was located just outside of town with plenty of space around it. But there truly was no space. Cars were just abandoned in front of the hospital. Lining up on the berm of the road and then the driveway in no particular order. Ambulance drivers could not get close. They were pushing gurneys through the cars strewn across the driveway. Larry had no choice but to abandon his truck. He wasn't even sure he could open the door handle. He managed. The pain was too debilitating to even maneuver the handle.

He left his truck at the end of the driveway, in the grass, adding to the mess that was already there. Using his backside, he closed the door and staggered his way up the long driveway to the emergency entrance.

The emergency room was packed. Wall-to-wall people. Standing, sitting, taking a spot on the floor. All of them looking the same. Their arms, legs, faces marked with deep reddish-purple marks that were large and inflamed. Their bodies withered in pain. They trembled, moaned, cried for help. Some lay on the floor having fits of convulsions and some just lay on the floor not moving. Larry wasn't alone. Not in his suffering. Whatever was going on in his town and nearby city was bigger than Larry imagined. He knew he had to get help, he had to wait. He needed to get relief. He worked his way inside, finding a spot. Promising himself at the moment he felt even a little bit better he would leave and wait it out at home. Little did Larry know he would never go home. His journey ended there.

7.
KIT KAT

Cass guessed it wasn't what Walt expected to see when he walked outside his shop to talk to Lena.

Then again, no one in town was ever surprised at anything Ada did. But he couldn't keep his eyes off of her while she examined the wreckage of Brad's car.

"Well," Walt said, his eyes shifting to Ada. "I have good news and…"

Cass snapped her finger. "Finish."

"Engine is shot," Walt said. "I can rebuild, but I have to order parts. I can get a new one. But either way, this bus isn't going anywhere for at least a week. Unless you have it towed."

"No." Lena shook her head. "You can have my business. Cass says you're the best in town."

"Thanks," Walt replied. "I'm kinda the only one."

"Walt," Cass said. "You sure you aren't trying to take advantage of her celebrity?"

"What? No," Walt replied. "Think I'm making it up. Pop the hood, Cass, take a look, see for yourself."

Lena gasped. "Oh, you write and fix cars. So talented."

"Thanks."

"So what do you want me to do?" Walt asked. "Get a new one or...okay." He lifted his hand. "Why is Ada bent over sniffing the front end of the smashed car?"

"She's smelling deer guts," Cass replied.

"Why?"

"In case they're sour," Ada yelled over.

"I can goddamn guarantee," Walt yelled back, "after fourteen hours, they probably are."

"Smart shit." Ada walked over. "You can smell sickness, Cass, something is up, but it's not disease if that makes any sense. Let me research." Ada looked up to Walt. "You give her an estimate."

"Yeah, she needs to tell me what she wants me to do."

"Order a new one," Lena said.

"Do you need one of us to ride you somewhere?" Walt asked. "There's no car rental around here."

"What if I didn't go anywhere." Lena snapped her finger and turned to Cass brightly. "Is there anyone in town who knows how to run a camera, do some filming? Even if they don't have a camera, my phone is good. They just need to know how to block a shot. This place is great and everyone so quirky. I can do my show. Film it here, send it to my production team. Visit the locals, cook with them."

"They would love that," Cass answered. "That's what I love about your show." She then shook her head. "I don't know anyone."

"What about Kit's boy?" Walt suggested.

"Who's Kit?" asked Lena.

"Hot Cop," Ada said.

"That's right," Cass added. "I forgot about Kat."

"Wait." Lena held up her hand. "Hot Cop Kit has a kid named Kat?"

"Funny, huh?" Cass said. "Anyhow, yeah, he's actually good. He's the same age as...um, he's nearly seventeen. Not sure if his dad gave him back the camera after he was caught sneaking off to Seaver and uploading videos of people doing stupid shit in Griffin."

Lena laughed. "That's hysterical. I'll talk to Kit."

At the same time, Ada, Walt, and Cass said, "No!"

"Okay," Lena sang. "Why?"

Walt explained, "Kit has a thing against famous people. He's a single dad, has been for a while. His wife up and left them when Kat was two to go out to Hollywood to be famous."

Cass snickered. "We thought for sure she'd end up in porn."

Ada whistled. "Proved us wrong."

"Who is she?" Lena asked.

"Jennifer Blaine," Cass replied.

"What?" Lena asked in shock. "Maybe I should be the one to talk to Kit after I show him our social media wars. Her and I do not get along at..."

She didn't finish the sentence when the distant sound of sirens caught all of their attention and the three of them turned.

The sirens grew louder. It looked like a pursuit with flashing lights headed toward town. An expensive-looking SUV flew in and pulled over immediately. Seconds later, a squad car came to a screeching halt behind.

The siren was silenced, but the lights remained on as Kit stepped angrily from the police car, slammed the door, and stormed to the SUV which clearly carried two people.

Cass shifted her eyes to Lena who slowly lifted her phone. "Are you filming this?"

"Yes. I have to. This is great."

Kit held up his hand speaking strongly to the occupants, trying diligently to remain calm. "Don't even think about getting out of the car."

The window wound down revealing a rather meek-looking man behind the wheel.

"License and goddamn registration. Eight miles!" Kit blasted. "Eight fucking miles I chased you and you wouldn't pull over. Where the hell were you going in such a hurry and with such blatant disregard?"

"Here. Griffin," the driver said.

"You were coming here to this town?" Kit asked. "And you couldn't pull over any time beforehand. Did you not see me?"

"I did, sir," the driver said, "but we had to get here. You'll thank me."

"I'll...thank you? I should throw you in our jail until the County Judge comes."

"That's fine," the man said. "We're fine with that. As long as we're here in Griffin."

"And why is Griffin so important?"

"Well, you'll find out soon enough," the man said. "The world...the world as we know it. It's about to end."

Kit paused. "I see. And um...when is this going to happen?"

The man looked down to his watch. "No sooner than twenty minutes, no longer than eight hours. I know—wide window."

"It is," Kit said. "With the way you were rushing, I would think it's happening now."

"In some parts of the world."

"But not here?" Kit asked.

"We're good here," the man replied.

Kit nodded, stepped back, bobbed his head a few times, then approached the car once more. "License and registration."

"Wow," Walt exhaled and tapped Lena on the shoulder. "Looks like you picked a good time then to be stuck in Griffin."

Lena and Ada laughed at Walt's joke, making fun of the man's excuse to Kit.

Cass didn't.

Maybe it was the reporter in her or the bit of her father's curiosity that was embedded in her soul. But with the crazy deer and the sudden sickness, Cass truly had to wonder if maybe something really was going on and Griffin was so far removed, they were just blissfully unaware.

8.
SOMETHING OFF

Crete, Nebraska

Dr. Everette Caine was the chief resident at the hospital. He wasn't a hotshot, didn't pretend to know it all, but he was good with emergency medicine. Most of what they saw in the medical center were injuries and mild illnesses, nothing major.

He knew exactly what it was when he was called to the ER. He was taking a break and a nap in the quiet back room, when the head ER Nurse, Jan, barreled in.

"Caine, I don't mean to bother you," she said. "We have issues. People are just pouring in."

Caine sat up on the cot, trying to catch his wits. "Pouring in. Was there an accident?"

She shook her head. "They're sick."

Caine paused. "Sick?" he asked then started walking.

"Well, something, they range from mild to severe. Caine, I think we had a chemical attack."

It sent him into a panic and just before arriving at the emergency room, it hit him.

He knew exactly what it was.

Or believed he did.

He opened the chart on the computer for his first patient and looked at the symptoms. Inflamed skin, eyes burning, difficulty breathing.

"Jan, are they all like this?"

"Mild to severe."

"I know what it is. It's a reaction." He hurried over to the main board. He remembered hanging the flyer by it. It still remained and he took it from the wall. "They sprayed the entire county today. Twice in some parts. Everyone was told to stay inside and wait an hour."

"I find it hard to believe that this many people didn't listen," she said.

"I think they listened; I just think the advice was wrong. I think it lingered longer. I'll get…" He paused, looked at Jan, and his eyes cased her wrist. "Were you outside?"

She shook her head. "No, why?"

"You have a rash starting."

She glanced down to the small red patch on her wrist. "Strange. I did run out to my car. Damn it. But just for a second."

"Keep an eye on it." Caine then walked to the ER secretary and handed her the flyer. "Can you call this number, it's important, find out if anyone is reporting mass reactions to this bug spray."

"Absolutely, Doctor Caine."

He left the flyer with her, then made his way to the first patient. He could hear her calling the number, the beeping tones as she dialed and the recorded message that came over the speaker phone: "Thank you for calling the Department of Agriculture, Pred extermination division. At this time all lines are busy. Estimated wait time, six hours and three minutes."

Caine skid to a stop and glanced over his shoulder.

The secretary looked bewildered.

"Try once more then call Lincoln Memorial see if they have anything—if not, tell them we need help."

"Right away."

Confident it was handled, Caine squirted sanitizer on his hands, grabbed gloves, placed them on, and walked into the exam room. "Mrs. Rose, I'm Doctor Caine. Let's see what's going on with you."

Without a doubt in his mind it was a reaction. Her lips were swollen, as were her bloodshot eyes. There were, in places, splotches on her face, but her neck was red. Her chief complaint and discomfort were her arms.

Both had large patches of welting, purplish-red and raised. The skin appeared to be pulled so tight, burst blood vessels could be seen. Some of her rash bled and small lesions formed on the skin.

It was like nothing he had ever seen. For certain he would call for help because Caine just didn't know where to begin.

Seaver, Arizona

For an older guy, Sheriff Thomas considered himself pretty up on technology. He had the best computer system, and since he didn't protest the new cell tower, internet was never better.

He spent his days just keeping track of things that were going on in his town; in the summer months ahead he would deal with tourists that travelled through on the famed Route 66. Tourists that, while charmed by Griffin, wouldn't stay there because their technology was subpar.

He tried to tell them to spruce up, but the town refused.

Going to Griffin was like going back in time.

On a positive note, most of them couldn't read the stories on the internet when the scandal about the chief, for some reason, was all over the national news.

Thomas laughed.

Griffin was a strange town, so it made sense that the tour bus for some reality cooking show had pulled into his town with a camera crew. After that, the one and only cab in town dropped off the director and a bus driver.

Thomas saw it as a way to make things interesting in town, suggesting to them since the government initiative to eradicate the pred bugs was commencing forty miles west, they should stay put for the day.

The government was spraying—that wasn't untrue—but by the time they pulled into town, the 'stay inside for an hour' for that area was nearly over.

They agreed to stay which must have prompted creative juices. The director told Thomas that after lunch, if it was alright, he wanted to do some filming.

Thomas was all for that, even had Wesley at the motel give them cheap rates.

In the two hours since they'd arrived, they caused an excited buzz in town.

A positive one. It was nice to see.

He grabbed a slice of apple pie from the coffee shop and sat at his deputy's desk so he could watch the happenings outside.

The film crew were outside Frieda's bookstore.

He spotted Don 'Hillbilly Jim' Smith watching like a fanboy.

The delightful mixture of warm cinnamon and cold ice cream swirled in his mouth and, hating to do it, he rushed to swallow because the phone rang.

"Seaver Police, Sheriff Thomas speaking. How can I help you?"

"Hello, sir, this is going to be a strange call," the man on the other line said.

"Well, nothing is strange after this day. What can I do for you?"

"My name is John Feeny. I can't find or get a hold of my wife."

"When did you last see her?" Thomas asked.

"About three weeks ago."

"And you're just calling now."

"No. no," John said with a chuckle. "She's on the road with her television show."

Thomas raised his eyes to the window. "And she broke down?"

"Yes, last I heard she was in Griffin. A woman with a gun was at her bus door…"

"Crazy Ada," Thomas said. "She's not harmful. I think your wife's camera crew and director are here in Seaver."

"Yeah, she said they left her. But the phone went dead."

"That's Griffin for you. You're lucky you even got through at all on her cell," Thomas said. "Have you tried Griffin police?"

"I did. That's why I called you, no one answered."

Thomas laughed. "Yep, that's Griffin as well. And you figured, we're a nearby town."

"Exactly. I thought maybe you communicated with them," John said. "I know it's a weird request. But any way you can get through. I just want to make sure she's okay."

"Listen, I'll check, but I can assure you if she's in Griffin, she's fine. If they towed her vehicle to the shop there, she's in great hands. But like I said, I'll try to reach someone there. In the meantime, send a fax to Brass Balls and Beers."

"Sorry?"

"It's a local drinking hole there. I'll give you the fax. They love faxes. People fax their orders to them all the time. You fax you get ten percent. Weird shit."

"Thank you, Sheriff, I'll do that. Do you have the number?"

Thomas did. He gave it to John Feeny, reassured him once again his wife was fine, and he would do his part to help. After he hung up, he knew where to start. It would be with the director. Maybe he knew a way to get ahold of Mrs. Feeny.

A few bites left of his pie, Thomas looked down to the runny white of the ice cream. "Damn it, my vanilla bean melted." He hurried to eat the remainder, wiped his mouth, and stood.

Just as he opened the door, he felt a twinge to his ear, like he was bitten by a bug. Thomas flicked his ear, then scratched it as he walked outside.

"Hey." Don trotted over to him. "You're missing the fun."

"I was watching it. Anyhow, I need to talk to the director. I just got a call from John Feeny looking for his wife."

"Oh, wow. She's the star of the show. Her bus broke down. She stayed with it."

"That's what I figured. I mean, they wouldn't leave the woman there alone," Thomas said. "I think—"

Thud.

Thomas looked around. "Did you her that?"

"Yeah, what the hell?" Don peered around as well.

Thud.

It was a mystery quickly solved when another thud-thud not only occurred but hit Don on the head.

A dead bird.

After bouncing off his baseball cop, the bird joined the other two black birds on the ground nearby.

Thomas bent down to take a closer look. The wings were spread out, beak open, and it looked as if half its feet were missing.

"What the hell?" Thomas said.

"Probably got in a plane or something," Don said.

Not really convinced that was the right explanation, Thomas agreed with a 'probably' and looked up to the sky. It was clear and blue, and he couldn't see any other birds, nor did any more fall from the sky. Brushing it off as another weird thing for the day, Thomas thought no more about it and walked with Don to the film crew.

<><><><>

The Texaco sign was vintage and in pristine condition, as was the rest of the gas station. It was a relic from days gone by, kept up for appearances down to the style of the pumps and the vintage cars parked in the lot. The only thing not old-fashioned was the modern-day price of fuel.

It had a good view of everything.

It was set on the edge of town, with the police station directly across. Catty-corner from it was Eb's garage and across the street, just half a block away, was the ever-busy Brass Balls and Beer.

In between it all, the grocery store.

Other businesses and restaurants, along with the motel, were up the road farther east. But from a perfect vantage point, for Cass, Schmitty's was the place to be.

"So." Brian folded his arms, leaning against the 1957 Studebaker Silver Hawk. "What's the…well, no pun intended…scoop?"

"Eb didn't know there were two deer," Cass replied. "He said that the one that was in the grill smelled worse than death. Something was wrong. That was confirmed by Ada."

"And you're okay?"

Cass nodded. "I'm focusing on Marge and getting answers for her. See…" She nudged him. "I worked while you went to Seaver and had lunch for like three hours."

"Couldn't leave town. Had to stay in the diner," said Brian. "They were Pred dusting."

"Yeah, but not in Seaver."

"You know Thomas. Anything to show control." Brian reached down and scratched his forearm. "Damn it."

"Your psoriasis again?"

"Yeah, all freaking day. I have to get the cream. I should have got it in Seaver."

"You got something else. You saw the Feeny camera people show up in Seaver?" Cass asked.

"Oh, yeah. Where is she at now?"

"Staying with Ada, she's going to film Griffin while she's staying here. The show must go on. Then again, we have to see if Kit will let us borrow his kid."

"Kat." Brian nodded. "He was in my history class. He would do everything video. He'd love it."

"And that's why I'm waiting," Cass said. "To get permission from Kit. Whenever he finishes with the two strangers."

"Okay, he pulled them over in town?"

Cass pointed to their car. "Looks like a senior citizen dad and his middle-aged son. They zipped right into town to pull over."

"Saying they were running from the end of the world?"

"As we know it or something like that."

"Meanwhile"—Brian pointed—"they've been sitting in the chairs by the window for a half hour. Kit hasn't even talked to them."

"Because the chief isn't there and Kit is making them wait. But they don't care."

"Hold up." Brian stood upright and stepped from the car. "They're leaving the station."

Cass watched. They had to be father and son, they resembled each other in build and look. They even walked the same. She expected that they had been released and would head to their car. Instead, they kept walking.

"Are they're headed to…?" Brian asked.

"Looks that way."

Brian cringed. "Ouch, he's really making them pay."

"Wait out the punishment…at Brass Balls and Beer." Cass nodded watching the duo walk in there. "Okay." She nudged Brian. "Now's your chance."

"My chance for what?"

"Get the scoop from them. Find out what they're up to and why they're running. I mean they think the world as we know it is coming to an end. We need to find out."

"You're being facetious."

"A little," Cass said.

"You're the next Scoop, you do it."

"I'm on the crazy sick deer story so…"

Brian looked at her. "Cass?"

"Brian, what if they're connected?"

"Oh, I doubt that."

"One way to find out. Take the lead."

"Why me?"

"You're human interest," Cass said.

"No, I'm the obit guy."

"Still human interest."

"You're right." Brian nodded. "Let's do this. Let's talk to the mysterious strangers."

Cass walked with Brian across the street. It was his story, but she was willing to bet she'd do most of the questioning.

Stepping inside Brass Balls and Beer wasn't anything unusual for anyone that lived in Griffin. It always looked the same. Nothing ever changed. Same decor that was probably there fifty years earlier. Dim wall lights made to look like lanterns hung by the booths that lined the walls, and hanging lights with a long, colorful oval shade dangled over the bar.

It was dim, no matter what time of day or night.

In typical audible fashion, Frank Sinatra played on the jukebox.

Usually when someone entered, they'd go to the bar. There they'd get a menu or order a drink, or pick up an order they had faxed in.

Cass spotted the two strangers sitting in the middle booth. A bowl of peanuts between them as they nursed their glasses of beer.

Neither of them talking.

"Why don't you find out from Glen what they're drinking," Cass said. "Get us a pitcher, and I'll meet you over there."

"Whew, so you're gonna make the first approach?" Brian asked.

"It'll be easier. They look lost and upset."

"Whether it's true or not, they think the world is ending," Brian told her. "How do you think we'd look if that was us? In a strange town, no one believing us, waiting for the kangaroo hearing to start."

"Kangaroo is appropriate. Our magistrate sucks."

"Yeah, well, we share him with Seaver. They suck."

"But they have good food," Cass said.

"Oh, the best ribs ever. Don't say anything at the diner."

"Promise," Cass whispered, her eyes locked on the two men. "Go ahead. Meet me at the booth."

"What if they tell you to go away?"

"Please," Cass scoffed. "I got this."

With a slight lean to her walk, head tilted, Cass made her way to the booth with the two men. Up close, they looked even more like fish out of water in Griffin. They certainly didn't look like tourists. The older man had thick salt-and-pepper hair that was combed rather neatly. His chest was slightly barreled and he wore a button-down denim shirt. The outline of a pack of cigarettes was in his pocket.

The younger of the two sat across from him and wasn't all that young. They were either father and son or brothers with a huge age gap. They were related without a doubt: the nose and chin were dead-on similar. The younger was a man in his forties, with wire glasses, hair similar to the older man's, only gray at the temples. He wore his combed down and parted extremely to the right like he was trying to comb over the bald spot the older man didn't have. His shirt was checkered and in his front pocket was a pocket protector. It made Cass laugh. The younger of the two was like the younger nerd version.

Smiling, Cass lifted her hand and cheerfully said, "Hi."

They both turned and looked at her at the same time. Both the same way with matching dumbfounded expressions that screamed *why are you talking to us?*

"Okay, weird," Cass said. "I had this weird flashback to *Terminator* and the human robots. Older model." She nodded at the older gentleman. "Younger. Can we join you?"

Both men in sync peered out of the booth.

"Like *Men in Black*," she said. "I'm Cass." She held out her hand

"Arthur…" He paused. "Smith. And this is my father, Bill."

"Smith?" Cass asked. "For real or is that a *Men in Black* joke?"

"*Men in Black* joke," Bill answered. "He's afraid you'll recognize his name. Please sit. Join us."

Cass slid in next to Bill. "Recognize huh? Are you famous?"

"I've been in the news a lot lately," said Arthur. "Not for anything illegal."

"Of course not. I actually work for the paper. I promise this isn't for an interview. So what is your…" She paused and looked up when Brian returned. "Where's the pitcher?"

"Glen said he will bring it over once he figures out what to do with the fax from John Feeny."

"John Feeny?" Bill asked. "The actor?"

Brian nodded. "Apparently the sheriff of Seaver told him to fax here."

Cass clarified. "We lose cell and Wi-Fi all the time here."

Brian continued. "And Glen doesn't know what to do with it."

"Oh." Cass leaned out of the booth. "Hey, Glen, she's staying with Ada. Fax him back and tell him and I'll deliver that to Ada's. I'm headed there in a bit."

"Sure thing," Glen replied. "I'll put it in an envelope for privacy."

Arthur crinkled his brow. "That is odd."

"Yeah, it's Griffin," Cass said. "Brian, sit. This is Arthur and his father Bill."

Arthur held out his hand. "Art, please, call me Art."

"Art," Brian greeted him, then his father.

"He is using the alias Smith. What is your last name?" Cass asked. "I may know it."

"You probably will if you're the press," Art said. "Bohr."

"Oh, like in Niels?" Cass asked.

"Niels?" Brian asked.

"Yeah, Niels Bohr, a physicist, won the noble prize in 1922. He was like very instrumental with understanding the atom and introducing us to quantum. You related?"

Bill nodded. "Yes. My great-grandfather's brother."

"Your great-grandfather is Harald?"

Art produced a quirky smile. "How do you know all this?"

"I'm a geek. But I don't recognize your name like you think I should. And lucky for you I can't look you up online right now."

"Good." Art smiled.

"So, Mr. Bohr. I saw you and your dad pull into town," Cass said. "I have never seen an entrance like that."

"Really?" Arthur asked.

"I also heard." Cass folded her hands on the table. "I'm curious. How is the world as we know it about to end?"

Arthur smiled. "You know, that came out wrong."

"So the world isn't going to end."

Arthur shook his head and looked at his father.

"Bill, you think it is?" Cass asked.

"No. No. Not at all."

"But you told Kit, the cop, you were headed right here, to Griffin, and that he'd thank you."

Art shrugged.

"And you implied Griffin was the only place to be."

"Not only."

"And that means?" Cass pushed.

"Art," Bill said, "she asks more questions than that officer."

"What did Kit ask?" Cass questioned.

Art shook his head. "Nothing really. He made us wait, then said not to leave town. Which we won't. We're going to try to get a room at that motel."

Cass bobbed her head. "That'll be easy. It's empty this time of year. So…The reason you gave for blowing him off for eight miles?"

"A bad excuse," Art said. "Like saying you were speeding because you have to go to the bathroom." He nervously chuckled. "You really didn't think I meant the world is going to end, did you?"

"'As we know it,'" Cass said. "Those were your words."

"I'm sorry," Art said. "I am. Especially if you thought you were getting a story."

"Not me. Him." Cass pointed to Brian. "He made me ask you the questions. He's the human-interest story guy. I'm glad to know the story isn't true and the world isn't going to end."

"As we know it," Brian added.

Cass smiled and pointed to Brian, then turned serious. "Look, Art, Bill, I'm sorry if we're coming across pretty crappy and cynical. I guess if I made it light, you'd feel more comfortable. But I can see that I just annoyed you."

Bill twitched his head once to the right. "She's good. Picking that up."

Cass gave a polite smile. "I can accept that. I didn't mean to come off strong." She looked up when Glen set down the pitcher and the sealed envelope with Lena's name on it. "Enjoy the beer." She stood, grabbing the envelope. "Welcome to Griffin. Brian, you ready?"

Brian stood.

"If you guys will excuse me." Cass placed the envelope in her pocket. "If I don't see you, best of luck. I have a vacation to pack for. I leave this evening. Nice meeting you."

She walked to the door with Brian.

Brian paused as he pushed open the door and whispered, "What was all that about?"

"My Hail Mary pass," Cass returned the whisper. "Hopefully it will be caught if I'm right…"

"Cass," Art called out.

"There it is. Go on," Cass said. "I'll fill you in."

Brian nodded and walked out.

Cass turned around to see Art had trotted to her.

"Look," Art said, "I can't say much only because I don't want to sound insane. But I'll tell you enough to keep you in town. Deal?"

"Deal." Cass walked back to the table.

9.

STRANGELY WEIRD

Route 66, Arizona

There was something about driving down Route 66, window all the way down, hot desert air flowing in while Chris Isaak's "Wicked Game" blasted on the radio. That was heaven for Griffin's Chief of Police, Carl Stanton.

It had been a nice day off, even if he had to go into the next county to help his cousin with the removal of the dead pred bugs. It was hard work, but interesting. Carl wasn't a young man, wasn't old either, but the crunching sound beneath his feet as he shoveled them made him laugh like he was a kid again.

It was satisfying. Maybe because the pred bugs were such a bad thing.

His cousin didn't even have a farm. He had a garden. A few berry bushes. But he was so inundated with them: they not only destroyed his garden, but his grass and trees too, and had coated his roof, which was not normal behavior for them. They didn't touch all the berry bushes though; it was like they were saving them for later.

The pred bug hotline had been called and, fortunately, the area would be covered by the morning's spray.

Carl worried about that, even doubted that it would work considering they were spraying thirty miles west. The hotline assured them it would carry.

Sure enough, it did.

They went from hearing the clacking of the bugs to complete silence.

Music to their ears.

Carl hated those bugs and was glad Griffin didn't have them, nor did Seaver. His current destination before heading home.

The heat and work caused him to have a headache, and he set his sights on stopping at Frieda's for a slice of pie and an ice-cold glass of her special tea.

A few miles out from Seaver, Carl felt a rumble in his gut. The headache was causing him to get sick. Sun-induced migraines usually did. He hadn't eaten much of anything. A half sandwich on his cousin's porch when they took a break from cleaning preds.

It got to the point that the bottle of water he kept sipping wanted to come up.

Before it did and caused a mess in the car, he pulled over.

"Oh, boy." Carl huffed a breath as he felt his stomach increasingly feel full. A sensation he knew only preceded vomiting.

Get it out, he thought. *I'll feel better.*

The knot grew, the swarming feeling of nausea was overwhelming. He could feel the sweat beading on his forehead, and he made his way to the side of the road, fully expecting to hurl.

It didn't happen.

He still felt sick. Half bent over, he opened his mouth, trying to get it out, but all that happened was a gagging reflex, some massive drool, and watering eyes.

He waited a few minutes. Perhaps it was because his stomach was empty. He didn't know, but the unproductive attempt of regurgitation left him feeling worse.

Three miles to Seaver.

Go there. Take a break. Hit the pharmacy for some antacid.

He walked back to his still-running car and slid into the driver's seat, grabbing his water bottle. He took a couple of hard, quick drinks while he closed the door and pulled the bottle from his mouth, feeling that uncomfortable lump roll down his esophagus from drinking too much, too fast.

He cringed some, using the back of his hand to wipe his still watering eyes.

Just as he brought the bottle back to his mouth to take a drink, he saw the blood on the back of his hand.

"What the hell?"

Not only was there blood on his hand, there were drops swirling around the remaining water in the bottle.

Slightly panicked, Carl reached for the rearview mirror and angled it his way to see his reflection.

Where he expected wet streaks to be from his eyes, he saw red…blood.

Still looking at his reflection, Carl opened his mouth. His teeth, tongue, even lips were blood stained.

He put the lid back on the bottle, tossed it to the seat, threw the car in drive and took off.

Three miles.

Three miles to Seaver and he'd get help.

Carl didn't need to be a doctor to know something was terribly wrong with him.

<><><><>

Cass sat in one of the four old wooden chairs in the waiting area of the police station. Her back to the window while she watched Kit and waited. Much like Art and Bill had done.

He looked constipated. His face tensed with frustration and wanting, but Cass knew what caused it. Kit was staring at the screen, wishfully thinking and hoping that page on the internet would load.

"You know," Cass said, "it's like boiling water."

"Shh."

"You can't watch the pot."

"Shh."

"And my speaking does what to slow down the dial-up even more?"

"Cass, please. I'm frustrated, I wouldn't have started to read that article had I known there was a next page."

"Did you disable images?" Cass asked.

"Yeah, but it's slow right now. Really slow."

"I understand your frustration. It was back this morning but I missed it. What's the article about?"

"Sports."

Cass laughed. "We have a sports page."

"You cover little league, Cass. Totally different thing. What did you want? You know you're not supposed to be in here."

"Again I will correct you," Cass said. "I'm not supposed to be here when the chief is here."

"He'll be here soon."

"Then I'll leave. I don't know why you carry such a grudge about that," Cass said.

73

"Because it disrupted the entire police station, Cass," Kit said as he walked from behind his desk.

"Because you lost his assistant."

"She quit because she was embarrassed."

"I would be too if everyone knew I'd slept with the chief."

"Stop."

"Oh, you know it's true," Cass said. "She quit because it came out."

"And we lost two officers over it," Kit said.

"Because, like you, they knew what that disgusting bastard was up to."

Kit huffed. "You are so argumentative. No wonder you keep getting married over and over."

"Hey, now, I have been married twice and Mark doesn't count."

"What do you mean he doesn't count?" Kit asked.

"I never even slept with him."

"Oh." Kit cringed. "Don't tell me your personal and private business I don't…" He paused. "You didn't sleep with your husband?"

"No, it was a strict business arrangement. I needed insurance. I needed to go away and get well. You know that."

"I thought he divorced you because of that."

Cass shook her head. "Our mayor is a really good guy. He knew I wasn't covered under Eb's any longer. County has really good benefits. He didn't ask for anything in return except never to bad mouth him and always have his back. Which is a given."

"Wow, I didn't know that."

"Now you do."

"Why are you here, Cass?" Kit asked. "Other than to stare at me while I wait for my internet pages to load."

"Can I borrow your son?"

"For what? You need some work done at your house?"

"No." Cass shook her head. "That TV reality celebrity is in town. She wants to film her show while she's waiting on her repairs."

"What's her show about?" Kat asked

"Cooking. She meets with local small-town folks and they share recipes and cook strange things. She needs a cameraman. Can I borrow him?"

"Yeah. But…" Kit waved a finger. "You're responsible for him. No bad influences from a celebrity."

"I promise." Cass held up her hand.

"Now, if you'll excuse me…"

"One more thing."

"What, Cass? What? I really want to read that article. There are things happening in this world outside of Griffin."

"That's it," Cass said. "The thing I need to talk about. According to our visiting father and son, that's the very reason they are here."

"Oh, stop." Kit walked back to his desk and sat down. "You can't possibly believe them."

"And you don't?"

"No!"

"Then why did you tell them not to leave town?"

"Because they blew me off for eight miles and the chief will have to deal with them."

"Did they say where they're from?" Cass asked.

"The father is from Texas. The son had a Baltimore license."

"See. See."

"See what?"

"They came so far. To escape to here," Cass said. "Why would they say it if it wasn't true?"

"To get out of a ticket. Pull a ruse. Who knows? We're the perfect town to pull off a practical joke like that. We're shut off from the world, we can't jump online at any time to find out the truth."

"Who on earth plays a practical joke about the end of the world?" Cass snapped.

"Um…Orson Wells."

"Oh, stop. He was reading a story."

"He intended to scare people," Kit said. "They couldn't go online either."

"But Seaver can. Call the sheriff."

"And ask what? If he heard the world is coming to an end?"

"No. Ask if he heard anything about a plague."

"A…plague?" Kit asked with disbelief.

"Maybe not a plague. It infects like the plague," Cass rambled fast. "Skin. Lungs or stomach. It's a sickness. Maybe not. More of a thing."

"A thing," Kit repeated calmly.

"They were vague."

"I'd say so. If they said a thing is infecting people. What exactly did they tell you?" Kit asked. "Specifically."

"Well, I lied to them…"

"Of course."

Cass grumbled. "I told them I was leaving town and Art, the son, said not to. That something was going to happen, it would cause people to get sick and die. It wasn't a virus, but it was real and everywhere around the world was going to experience it. They used the word experience."

"But not Griffin?"

Cass shook her head.

"Did they say why we were safe?"

"They said there were several safe places. We were closest when they took off to run for safety. Something about it carrying in trade winds, jet streams. The dad has a map."

"Did you see it?" Kit asked.

"No. He said it's in his luggage."

"I'm sure."

"And that it would eventually dissipate but not without causing complete devastation."

"That's a pretty bold thing to say."

"You're being sarcastic."

"No, I'm not," Kit said. "I'm trying to understand why you believe them."

"I don't know if I believe them," Cass said. "They looked and sounded so serious. He asked how long the internet and cells would be down. I told them there's been times it was down for days. And Art said by the time it comes back up, there will be no one left to post."

"Griffin is safe. What about Seaver?"

"I asked that," Cass replied. "They said it was iffy. But they knew for sure Griffin was fine. So call Seaver. Have them go online and see if there's been any reports of strange illnesses or occurrences. I'd call but they won't take me seriously. I'd tell you to look it up online, but—"she pointed to the computer—"you're still waiting on the sports article."

Kit exhaled slowly and sat back, rocking some in the chair. "Fine." He leaned forward again and grabbed the phone.

"Thank you. Thank you very much. I'm going to head to your place to talk to your son."

"He should be home. They didn't have school today." Kit dialed.

Cass walked to the door. "Let me know what they find out."

77

"Sure thing."

She looked back once more; the phone was to his ear. Cass walked out, stopped to fix her shoe, and looked in the window as she passed. She watched Kit hang up and she rushed back in. "What the hell, Kit? Was that a farce to shut me up? Wait until I leave then…" She noticed the look on his face, a far-off glance of concern. "Kit?"

Kit lifted the phone and dialed. "They didn't answer."

"The police department didn't answer? Well, we don't answer."

"Yeah but it transfers to county after six rings. This…" He hung up and redialed.

"Again, no answer?" Cass asked.

Kit shook his head. "No. But I'm sure it's something other than the end of the world. Go do what you were doing. I'll let you know."

"Thanks." Cass walked back to the door

"And, Cass," Kit called out to her.

Cass paused at the door. "Yeah?"

"I'm sure it's fine and…Hello, Sheriff? Yeah, Officer Modine, Griffin Police. Good. Good, how are you?"

Cass smiled and gave a thumbs-up, mouthing, "Let me know."

"Sheriff can you hold on?" Kit covered the receiver. "As soon as I hear anything."

Nodding a thanks, Cass, a bit more upbeat and relieved, walked out.

"Yes," Kit said. He watched as Cass walked by the window and waved. Once she was out of his sight, and knew he was out of hers, Kit hung up.

The sheriff was never on the line, again, there was no answer.

Maybe it wasn't right to deceive Cass like that. But the last thing Kit wanted was for Cass to get scared, and start worrying others, especially when she was on her way to get his son.

There was an explanation for the lack of answer in Seaver, and Kit was certain he'd find out what that was as soon as he got through to them.

<><><><>

The motel didn't really have a name. The sign said 'motel' and that was good enough for Bill and Art Bohr.

While Art was inside room eight, Bill stood outside. His arm raised slightly, rested on the awning support beam while his fingers dropped down to his scalp. His head felt itchy—that was nothing new for Bill. Whenever he was tired, he always seemed to scratch.

He took the last draw of his cigarette, flicking it out to the parking lot at the same time the door opened.

He turned around. "Done?" Bill asked.

"Done," Art answered. "All clean. Nothing."

"Good."

"And uh…I think you can smoke in this room."

"Nonsense." Bill stepped inside. "I don't think a hotel in the country allows smoking."

"There's an ashtray." Art pointed and closed the door.

"Hot damn, I get to hear you bitch," Bill said. The room was typical hotel looking. Two beds, a dresser, television, and in the corner a small makeshift kitchen.

Bill plopped to the bed with the grace of a sack of potatoes.

"Tired?" Art asked.

"Yep. Today has been a whirlwind."

"You aren't kidding." Art sat on the other bed. "It couldn't be any other way though."

"No, it could not. We had to wait until the last minute."

"No room for error," Art said. "Even a couple miles can make a difference."

"You know it wasn't skill, right?" Bill asked. "I tried. It was more luck."

"Whatever or however you came up with the calculations you were right. Thank you."

Bill exhaled sharply. "When will we know for sure?"

"I'm ninety percent certain we are good. I'll do a check around town tomorrow morning, some of the obvious spots. But if nothing is there. We're good."

"And do you plan on telling anyone?" Bill asked. "You brought everything you need to prove it."

Art nodded. "I figure they'll need an explanation but I'll wait until they ask. Really the proof will be in leaving Griffin. Then they'll see."

"When will it be safe for them to do that. For us to leave?"

"Thirty-six hours from right now. But really, Dad, leave? We might as well stay. Because if I'm right, and I'm certain I am." Art stood up and paced. "There's really nowhere left for us to go."

<><><><>

It had to be the end of the strangest day. Cass was tired but not sleepy, and she couldn't with a clean conscious go home without stopping by Marge's place to give her an update on the accident story.

Cass tried to call Marge's house earlier in the day but there was no answer and Cass figured Marge was at the hospital with her son. So after a few hours at Ada's, watching Lena have a production meeting with Kat, Cass decided to stop by Marge's before she dropped off the boy. Fill her in about the sick deer story. How the deer was the reason for the accident.

Then again, if the two strangers in town were right, there were more ominous things happening. Cass wasn't convinced the strangers were lying. She also wasn't convinced that the deer that went rabid weren't infected with whatever 'thing' it was that Art and his father were running from.

Cass parked her car on the street by Marge's walk, leaving Kat in the car. She could see him in the front seat, slouching down, probably bored. Cass knocked on the door, rang the bell, and waited. The lights were on, yet there was no answer. She peeked through the window…nothing.

Finally, Cass gave up and returned to her car.

"Sorry about that," she said to Kat.

"No problem."

Cass smiled and looked at the boy. Sixteen, tall like his dad, but with a teenage boy build. His face so much like his mom's. "Are you hungry?" Cass asked. "I know you were hoping to try that cake you filmed her baking."

"Yeah, but I didn't have hours to wait."

"No, you didn't. Maybe you should have had some of Ada's chicken."

Kat shook his head.

"Brass Ball and Beer is still serving. Wanna burger?"

"No, but thank you. I have to get home. It's Hamburger Helper taco night."

"I'm sorry, Hamburger Helper and tacos?" Cass asked as she drove down the street.

"Something like that. With a veggie and green Jell-O."

"Wow, Kit goes all out," Cass said sarcastically.

81

"He tries. He does."

"I know. And I'll owe you that burger, how's that?"

Kat nodded.

It wasn't long before they arrived at Kat's house. Cass could drive from one end of town to the other in less than two minutes.

She got out of the car at the same time as Kat.

"You don't need to walk me," Kat said.

"Oh, I know. I need to talk to your dad. Tell him about me picking you up tomorrow and find out what his rules are."

"Rules?" Kat stopped directly before the porch.

"Yeah, I'm responsible for you."

"Like a babysitter?"

The front door opened and Kit stepped onto the porch. "Hey," Kit said. "How was it?"

"Good," Kat answered. "Dad, I don't need her to babysit."

"Oh, I know. You're a good-looking kid. I have her making sure that Hollywood woman doesn't try to get her claws into you." He opened the screen porch door. "Go inside. Wash up. Dinner is on the table in a second."

"Yes, sir."

Cass folded her arms and stepped onto the porch.

"Thanks for driving him back," Kit said.

"No problem. I wanted to talk to you. I'll be picking him up at ten tomorrow. He's gonna film Lena doing a garden episode. I'll make sure she doesn't…hit on him."

Kit smirked.

"What's my rules here, Kit? Can I leave him with Ada or do I need to be by his side?"

"He's fine if Ada is around. I just don't know this Hollywood person."

"Well, as it is a cooking show, maybe I'll introduce her to you since Kat wanted to rush home for this special meal you do."

"Hey, now don't knock my Monday Madness Meal day."

"So this is every Monday?"

"Yep." Kit nodded.

"Good thing for you she'll be in town another week. You may get your chance." Cass backed up. "I'll let you go. Have a good night."

"Cass. Did you…did you wanna stay for supper?" Kit pointed back. "You're welcome to. We have plenty."

"Kit, I don't ever think I've been in your house before. Or invited in."

"You're not the most social person you know. Or haven't been over the last few years."

"You're right," Cass said.

"But you gotta do what you gotta do to get through," Kit stated. "So what about staying. I know you're just gonna hit the BBB for a burger. Have a home-cooked meal."

"You really made green Jell-O?"

"Every Monday."

"Then thank you. I think I will."

Kit opened the screen door for her. "On one condition."

"What's that?"

"No talk of sick deer, car accidents, the indiscretions of the chief of police, or end of the world."

"Good lord, Kit." Cass walked into the small house. "You just scratched off all of my hot topics. What am I gonna talk about?"

"How about for starters, how much you're gonna love"—Kit showed her the kitchen table—"Hamburger Helper tacos." He pulled out a chair. "Sit down. I'll get a place setting for you." He backed away and hollered, probably forgetting Cass was so close. "Kat! Now! Dinner!"

His loud voice made Cass jump a little, but then she laughed. She looked at the dinner set out on the table. Sure enough Hamburger Helper inside of taco shells.

It smelled good. Cass wasn't sure how it would taste, but she knew one thing: the long day with odd events had been triggering things she hadn't had triggered in a while, and dinner with the Kit-Kat combo, delicious or not, would be a perfect diversion.

10.
SPOTTED

May 6

Crete, Nebraska

It was his duty to do what needed to be done. Niles Proctor arrived at the fourth hospital in twenty-four hours. The British-born doctor had been in Lincoln when the call came from the small university hospital in Crete. But he saw it on the bulletin board.

A simple notice if anyone had time to help out.

He knew no one had time.

Niles did.

He used that final text message from a colleague as inspiration to go on. He couldn't right the grievous wrong he played a role in, but he could do what needed to be done to try to make up for it, and to also ease his own guilt.

Guilt that was genuine but unnecessary. Everything he and his colleagues had done was for the betterment of mankind, to save mankind. No malice whatsoever, but any good they'd done had been overshadowed in the previous forty-eight hours and they were perceived as opportunists.

Niles was a tall man, slender in build. Thick dark brown hair with a dash of gray here and there.

People who knew him called him distinguished; they said he spoke that way. Niles laughed it off saying they were American and all British folk sound distinguished compared to them.

In his car, just outside the packed driveway before the hospital, Niles looked down to that text message.

"We failed," it read. "It proceeds despite our best efforts. Please get to a safety zone ASAP, there's nothing left to do."

Niles disagreed.

He had plenty left to do.

He knew well what he was facing and what was coming. He prepared to face that, not hide and protect his own life. He did, in a sense, his best to stay safe and not run.

He donned a protective suit he'd taken from the lab, plenty of oxygen packs, and began his road trip.

Before stepping out of his car, he placed down his phone and grabbed the hood to his suit.

He stepped from his car, connecting the oxygen, checking his levels, then placed on the head covering. He went to the back of his SUV where he grabbed a pair of gloves, booties, and duct tape, then carefully sealed his wrists and ankles.

Lifting his case from the back end, Niles made his way to the hospital.

With each place he stopped it was both progressively worse and better.

Better because there wasn't as much suffering.

He walked into the hospital. It was quiet. No movement, no sound.

Slowly, Niles walked up to every single person there. Whether they lay on the floor of the waiting room, on a gurney in the hall, or slumped over their desk.

He examined and checked them.

He looked at the devastation upon them. A skin rash so raw that flies darted in and out. Some lay on their sides, bloody vomit expelled from their wide-open mouths.

There wasn't a single case there that wasn't unique in some way—the route of transmission was different for everyone.

All evident upon seeing them.

"Help...me," a weak voice called out.

Niles turned to where the sound had come from. Two gurneys up the hall he saw a twitching arm. He rushed to the woman. Her face completely covered in the rash, she coughed, expelling droplets of blood.

"Help."

"I will. I'm here. I'll help," Niles said, giving a reassuring grip to her arm before lifting the lid to his case. Inside he had hundreds of prepared syringes. He used less each place he went. He retrieved one from the case and tried as best as he could to convey a compassionate look to the woman as he injected the syringe into her arm. "I'm very sorry this happened to you. Rest."

He waited with the woman until she closed her eyes, then her labored breathing slowed to a halt.

Nile moved on.

He felt like a revolutionary soldier on the battlefield, going through the injured soldiers, one by one, and putting them out of their misery.

That was what he did.

A doctor of death.

Only Niles felt he was a doctor of death days before the 'dusting' went bad.

He would walk the entire Crete hospital, then disinfect and move on.

He'd stop at every facility on his way to his destination, realizing that in twelve hours it would be in vain. He'd still do it.

Niles was certain there were plenty of places to check on his way to Griffin, Arizona.

<><><><>

When Ada first saw them, she didn't know what to say. Were they actually food? A pot pie size nest made out of hash brown potatoes, lined with sausage and an egg was in the middle. But that wasn't all.

It was a bountiful breakfast laid out. So much food she was glad that Eb stopped by to give an update on the bus. At least he'd eat.

"What did you do?" Ada asked Lena. "Stay up all night."

Lena chuckled. "Oh, no. I do this all the time. Not to this extreme. But it's all a matter of timing. You can get this all done in ninety minutes. Not bad at all. I wanted to show you what you could serve if you made this a bed and breakfast."

"This is amazing," Eb said. "The coffee is out of this world."

"It's store brand," Ada replied.

"No," Lena said. "I had that in my bag."

"Really?" Ada rushed to the coffee pot. "Then I have to try."

"I'll get it for you. Sit. Eat," Lena instructed. "Cass, Kat, and Brian will be here soon."

"Why Brian?" Eb asked.

"Cass said something about her wanting him to do a real human-interest story." Lena shrugged.

Eb nodded knowingly. "Yeah. Brian is known for his creative obituaries."

"He's good," Ada said. "Did you read the obituary he did on Mrs. Stevens, the history teacher?"

"Oh my God, yes," Eb replied. "Three times."

Ada accepted her coffee with a thanks. "Lena, if you did all this what is Kat gonna film?"

"I thought we could film the garden and you can explain your technique."

"You mean put me on the TV?" Ada asked.

Lena nodded.

"No. Not this old face." Ada sipped her coffee. "This is good."

"Glad you like it. I can get you camera ready. You'll look twenty years younger."

"That's something to think about. Maybe Brian won't be so ready to write my obituary."

Cass' voice entered the kitchen. "Brian isn't coming. He texted me last night said he wasn't feeling well. I think he's just embarrassed because his psoriasis is acting up."

Ada cringed. "He does get it bad."

"Must be something in the wind," Lena said. "John's fax said he and the girls have poison ivy."

"It's that time of year," Eb said.

Cass peeked at the food. "This looks great."

"Have some," Lena told her. "I'm making Eb eat, he came to tell me about the bus."

"Be ready next week," Eb said, then looked at Kat as if he'd just noticed him. "Holy cow, Kat. You got tall."

"You'll have that," Kat replied. "Especially when your dad is tall."

"He is," Eb said. "How old are you now?"

"Sixteen. I'll be seventeen next month." Kat sat down at the table.

"Are you driving?" Eb asked.

"Just started."

"Wow." Eb sat back. "Time goes fast. You realize, Cass, Jordie would be driving now too."

"Yeah," Cass' voice cracked. "Can you excuse me. I have to get back to town."

She started to leave.

"Wait," Lena called. "Take your breakfast buffet muffin with you." She handed her one wrapped in a towel.

"Thank you." She passed a smile to Lena, lifted her hand in a slight wave, and hurried out.

"Was it something I said?" Lena asked.

"Nope," Eb answered. "Something I said." Eb slipped for a moment, was solemn, but quickly bounced back and resumed his conversation with Kat.

11.
NO MORE RUNNING

Brass Balls and Beer wasn't just a pub for happy hour and evening socializing, it was place to eat when those in Griffin just didn't want the atmosphere of the friendly family diner. Or in Kit's case, being in ear shot of too many people.

He ordered three coffees from Glen and said he'd let him know about breakfast. He wanted to see what his table companions wanted.

When Art and Bill arrived, they seemed relieved that Kit wanted to speak to them in less than legal surroundings, that the coffee was good, and the breakfast menu was still available.

Bill looked up to Glen when he set the plate of eggs down. "Thank you."

"So you're believing us," Art said to Kit.

"You're not telling me anything," Kit replied. "Really, other than see who left town, that could tell us something and set up a...road-block."

"Just for today," Art said. "Tomorrow will be fine."

"And are you going to tell me exactly what this...thing...as you put it, is?" Kit asked.

Art nodded. "I will once I know if I was right or wrong. There are a lot of variables and if I spew them out without visual proof as an explanation it won't make sense."

"Hmm," Bill hummed out. "Kind of early to be drinking. Or is that normal in this town?"

"Dad, I'm not drinking," Art said.

Kit saw Bill stare at the bar and when he looked over, he saw Cass. She sat center of the bar, a glass before her with an inch of brown liquid, more than likely whiskey. "Can you...can you guys excuse me?" Kit stood up.

Cass tapped her forefinger on the side of the glass steadily, causing the whiskey to ripple slightly. It was hypnotic, and she stared at it. Wanting to drown all in her mind, but there wasn't enough whiskey in the bar to do that.

For the second day in a row her mind couldn't stop thinking. Going back.

You realize, Cass, Jordie would be driving now too. Eb had said.

And just like that, Cass was back.

Their car was a mess and they'd only been on the road three hours. Food wrappers, empty coffee cups, and the car ashtray that fit in the cup holder was already overflowing. Eb chain-smoked when he drove.

They laughed, the radio went from off then on, but more so they watched her parents' blue sedan ahead of them. They stayed a few car lengths behind, following them on the family vacation.

"Fifty-seven," Eb said as they drove. "Whoa. Wait. Fifty-nine."

"He's creeping up to the speed limit." Cass laughed.

"Your father will never drive the speed limit. Ever."

"I don't know what changed," Cass said. "I remember my mother always yelling at him to slow down."

"He probably never sped," Eb told her. "Just not your dad. Your mom is probably still telling him to slow down."

"We should have been the lead car," Cass said.

"No, then we'd be doing that thing where we pull over every twenty miles to wait for them."

"We may get to the Grand Canyon this week, right?" Cass joked.

Eb laughed. "Oh, wait, he's picking up speed. No, he changed his mind. Fifty-six...shit."

Truck.

It came out of nowhere, full speed, appearing like a ghost from over the edge of the slight grade. It wasn't a tractor-trailer, it was a pickup truck. A newer one and bigger than normal. It was as if the driver didn't realize he had his own lane. He drifted into their lane and plowed head-on into her parents' car.

Just like that.

An instant, a split second. Laughter to heartache.

The blue sedan folded, smashed, and flipped like a box being clipped by a car going full speed down the road.

So fast. So hard.

Cass instantly and instinctively released a gut bellowing scream just before Eb's hard breaking caused the car to spin sideways and become one with the wreckage of the truck.

Everything went black.

She wished to God Eb wasn't such a good driver or his reaction time was a second slower—if it had been, she, too, along with Eb would have been dead.

"An old familiar scene," Kit said standing by her at the bar. He took a seat. "Stare, think, wait, drink it fast then go."

"Yep." Cass nodded. "Only I'm not washing down pills."

"That's a good thing," Kit said.

"You're not gonna ask me if I'm going to take them again, are you?"

"Have I ever?" Kit asked. "You stopped. That's good enough for me."

"Eight years, Kit. Eight years," Cass whispered. "And the memories I am having today and yesterday are as real as they were then."

"Cass, there is no time limit on grief. Especially loss when it's sudden and traumatic. This isn't the first time you flashed back there and it won't be the last. It's how you handle it."

"You're right."

"I knew…I knew putting you on that accident story wasn't a good idea."

"It was a trigger, but you know, but Eb…Eb today just innocently said that Jordie would be driving like Kat and"—Cass snapped her finger—"bam. There I was."

Eb's voice called to her. "Cass, Cass please, it's going to be alright."

She was outside, the sun blaring in her eyes when she came to. On her back, she knew she was being carried and Eb moved with her, running alongside the stretcher, the sound of the helicopter whirling loudly. "Eb. Eb…are they…?"

"Cass, we're getting you help."

She saw his face. A streak of blood ran down from his brow. "Eb." She sobbed. She didn't feel any bodily pain. She didn't even know why they were taking her. Her head turned the other way and when she did, she saw her parents' car, a small fire smoldered up front. On the ground next to it she saw two covered bodies. Both of them small. "No!" she screamed.

Just like that everyone she loved was gone.

It didn't matter how careful of a driver her father was, he wasn't in control of the others on the road. She blamed herself for telling the kids they could ride with her parents. Her oldest daughter, Jordie, was eight at the time, her youngest, Layla, was four. It didn't matter what Eb said. She felt guilty. It wasn't just the loss that tore her and Eb apart, it was Cass. She just couldn't accept that she witnessed their deaths, never got to say goodbye, and never died with them that day.

"He can say things like that," Cass told Kit. "With a smile. Me...no. I mean, yeah, I think of the girls and the memories and smile but...back then. He was strong."

"He was broken, Cass," Kit said. "He just threw himself into work. We do what we need to do to get through. You did what needed to be done."

"But Eb did it the right way."

"Is there a right way?"

Cass just looked at Kit. "Maybe not. But we can say there's a wrong way." She peered down for a second to her drink. "I didn't just want to die that day, I wanted to die back then. I tried."

"Oh, I know."

Everything was blurry. How many pills had she taken? How much booze had Cass drunk? The road felt rippled and sideways when it wasn't. On the dark highway, the bright headlights of the tractor-trailers glared in her double vision. The only thing that was clear was the sound of the long warning horns that sounded off every time a truck avoided hitting her.

A double blip-blip of a police siren and Cass stopped.

She turned around swaying, shielding her eyes from the flashing lights.

"Cass!" Kit shouted to her and raced her way. "What the fuck are you doing?" He grabbed hold of her arm.

"Leave me alone, Kit, I just want to die." She pulled her arm away.

"You don't think drinking and popping pills won't eventually get you there?"

"Not fast enough." She brough the bottle to her lips.

Kit grabbed the bottle and threw it. "Not on my watch, Cass. If you don't care enough about yourself, care about Eb. Don't do this to Eb."

"He already divorced me."

"He still loves you. I will not let you do this to him. Now, let's get in the car…" He reached again for her. "Get you back home and—"

"No!" Cass yanked away, spun, and backed away. "Let me do this, Kit. You're not stopping me." She tried to run, staggering some. She saw the lights of the oncoming truck and she walked right to it.

"You tased me," Cass said, then after a beat she softly chuckled. "I can't believe you tased me."

"Gotta do what you gotta do."

"Have I ever thanked you for saving my life that day?" Cass asked.

"Yeah, you did. You hit rock bottom, Cass, all of us knew you'd make a change once you did that. My Taser had nothing to do with it. I'm glad you stopped wanting to die."

"Yeah, me too. It's my way to keep them alive," Cass said. "You know some ancient something or other says a person lives as long as someone is around to remember them."

"I think that's *Westworld*," Kit said.

"Or the movie *Coco*." Cass smiled and looked over her shoulder. "So, I see you're meeting with our newcomers. Is it official police business?"

"No, just talking. They still aren't specific. They still say we're safe. They want me to ask around to see if anyone left town yesterday at all. You know, see if they're showing signs of this…thing, whatever it may be. Did you, Cass," Kit said with joking tone, "leave town?"

"Not me. Well, Miller Run Road, but that's not out of town. Brian went to Seaver."

"Brian went to Seaver?"

"Yeah, for lunch yesterday with Patty. They were there for a while," Cass replied.

"Where is he now?"

"Get this," Cass said. "You'll crack up. He's sick or something." She noticed Kit immediately looked over toward Bill and Art. "Kit, he's fine. You talked to Seaver yesterday, they're a safe place."

Kit looked at her.

"You did talk to Seaver, right?"

Kit didn't answer.

"Goddamn it, Kit, you lied?"

"Well, Cass I just didn't…"

"Son of a bitch." She slammed her hand and stood up.

"Where are you going?"

"To check on Brian." She lifted her drink, downed it, swiped up her keys, and stormed out.

Kit tossed up his hands after she flew by him. "And she drinks and drives."

Cass was on Brian's porch at the front door when she heard the call of her name.

"Cass, wait!" Art called out.

She turned around. Kit, Art, and Bill were walking toward her.

"Don't go in there," Art said. "Not alone."

"Cass," Kit scolded. "You flew here, downed a double shot, you know at your body weight…"

"Shut up, Kit, it's not even in my blood stream yet," she snapped. "Something is wrong. I called. I knocked. I tried the back door. He's not responding. Drapes are drawn, I can't see in."

"He's obviously home." Kit pointed to the car in the driveway.

"No shit." Cass tried the front door. "Locked. Can you break it down or something?"

"Hold on." Kit ran back to the police car, popped the trunk, and reached in. He returned to the door with a Halligan bar.

Cass stepped out of his way.

Kit wedged the bar in the door and with a grunt pulled to pry the lock. The door opened.

As soon as the sunlight entered the dark home, Cass saw Brian on the floor.

"Oh my God." She ran to him. "Brian."

"Don't touch him." Art shouted. "Don't touch him. Please. Wait."

"Is he contagious?" Kit asked.

"Not him so much as what might be on him." Art pulled out a pair of rubber gloves from his pocket. "Don't touch anything in this house. Not yet."

"I'll put the light on," Kit said.

"Not yet. Don't draw the drapes." Art crouched down and gently felt for his neck. He shook his head. "He's gone."

"What?" Cass asked in shock. "What happened to him? Look at him."

Even though it was dark, Cass could see what looked like fresh wounds on his arms and around his mouth.

Art carefully removed the rubber glove, placed on another and from his front check pocket pulled out what looked like a pen light. It was, but it was a black light. He aimed it at Brian's mouth and chin. The light exposed bright spots, some round, some looking like clouded smear marks. He ran the light down to his hand and it was the same there. "Subcutaneous route of infection," Art said. "He touched it. It was on his hands, his arms, he touched his face, probably a secondary inhalation exposure as well. This"—he pointed—"is what we were running from." He slowly stood up. "There's no running anymore."

<><><><>

In the immediate aftermath of the discovery of Brian's and Patty's bodies, Kit was lost. He rattled questions to Art in an angry manner. "Do we have a biological hazard here?"

"In a sense."

"In a sense? So this is all highly contagious."

"Only if you touch it and only for another twenty-four hours. That should kill it."

"Jesus." Kit paced. "So I don't call county. Just leave the bodies here in the middle of the living room to rot."

"There's no one to call."

The call Kit wanted to make at that moment was bullshit. To him there was no way, no how, no one was around and gone that fast. It wasn't possible.

Since they couldn't do anything about Brian and Patty, Kit cranked up the AC as high and cold as it could go and requested everyone go back at the police station.

Cass was the last one to enter. "Okay, I stopped by Doctor Holloway's home," she said as she walked in. "He'll be here momentarily."

"Did you stop anywhere else?" Kit asked. "Tell anyone else."

"You mean did I go to Ada's?"

Kit nodded.

"No."

"Okay, because you took a while."

"Oh, I stopped at Brass Balls for another shot."

"Cass."

"What?" She pulled out a chair and joined them around Kit's desk. "It's the end of the world." She glanced over at Art and Bill. "'As we know it.' Other than the doc, are we waiting for anyone else? The chief because I think this situation warrants me being allowed to break the restraining order."

"You have a restraining order against the chief of police?" Art asked.

"Oh, no, he has one against me. Long story."

"Yes," Kit said. "We won't get into it. The chief…I was unable to get ahold of him."

"Where was he?" Art asked.

"West. He was helping his brother all day."

Bill nodded. "So he's dead."

"We don't know that," Kit snapped. "I tried Seaver. Maybe their communications are down. I need to go there…"

"Not yet," Art said. "Tomorrow. Not before."

Kit tossed out his hands. "I wish to God you'd tell me what you know."

"I will. When the doctor gets here, so I won't have to explain it more than once."

The old-fashioned ding-a-ling bell rang and a younger man walked in. He wasn't much older than thirty. Deliberately shaved bald head, and thin.

"Hey, Doc," Kit said.

"He…" Bill pointed. "Is the town doctor? Looks so young. I pictured some older guy."

Cass shook her head. "We don't have an old town doctor. We have a county PCP that comes in. Sets up shop. They do like a three-

100

year tour of duty. No one stays. They send us residents fresh from the hospital. We know when we get a new pastor a new doctor isn't far behind."

The young doctor shook Bill's and Art's hands. "You can call me Craig or Doc. Whichever you prefer. What's going on?"

"Pull up a chair," Kit instructed. "We have a situation on our hands."

"Since you called me, I am assuming it is of a medical nature," Craig said.

"Wide scale," Art told him. "Global."

"Is it here?" Craig asked. "In Griffin?"

"In a way," Art explained. "There are a lot of variables involved. They wouldn't have been exposed to it here. But if they were out of town yesterday. Were you out of town yesterday?"

"Yes," Craig said. "I was northeast yesterday morning doing rounds at the hospital. I was back here before noon."

"Then you're fine," Art said. "Anyone west of here after ten a.m. and anyone east of here after three p.m. are in danger."

"What about north and south?" Cass asked.

Bill answered. "Noon."

"But the thing is," Art said, "if they were affected, they would have symptoms now. Has anyone called you with symptoms like a bad rash, trouble breathing, severe burning when breathing, stuff like that?"

"Got two calls yesterday about rashes."

"Was Brian one of them?" Cass asked.

"Yeah, and the other was Mrs. Sanders."

"This is important," Art said. "Did you see them? Examine them?"

101

Craig shook his head. "No. I didn't. I just told them to use a topical or Benadryl if the itching was too much. They could get both at the grocery. So I take it this is highly contagious and lives on a surface?"

"It does," Art said. "But not for long. You can't…shed it like a normal virus. It doesn't carry in droplets. It does carry in blood. It transfers from hand to surface—the longer it is on the skin, the more it loses strength. Outside of Griffin right now, it will run out of hosts and die off by tomorrow. We just need to find anyone and everyone that's left. Stop people from leaving. Check any place they may have stopped or been."

"Disinfect?" Kit asked.

"No. Disinfectant won't kill this. Time does, that's the only thing. Close the establishment if we see it with a black light. Twenty-four hours."

"Fuck," Cass blurted out. "Brian was at Brass Balls and Beer."

"Then you'll be happy to know it's clean," Bill said. "My son checked it last night. The bartender was very nice about him doing that. We told him it was an experiment."

"On a positive note," Art said, "it really isn't that easy to transfer to a surface. An affected person really needs to be exposed to that surface for a while and steadily. Just stopping in the store won't do it."

Craig waved out his hand and facially showed he was confused. "By no means am I a virus expert, but this thing sounds very different with a unique set of rules you seem to know very well."

"I do and sadly I should," Art said. "I created it."

12.
A BREEZE

"You're a scientist," Kit stated.

He reined in control when Cass and Craig both seemed to go off after Art took credit or responsibility for what was happening.

"Yes," Art answered. "A microbiologist. My specialty is mycology, study of fungi, bacteria, that sort of thing,"

Kit looked at Bill. "Are *you* a scientist, too?"

"No, no, no." He shook his head. "I'm a rancher. I just know weather patterns."

"And it's a good thing," Art said. "He and I wouldn't be alive if he didn't."

"I am so lost," Kit said. "What is happening?"

"Let me go back to the beginning," Art said.

"Please," Kit said.

"As you know the ladybug was an issue with crops. So the stinkbug was genetically manipulated to quell the ladybug problem. Then the stinkbug got out of control. Enter the pred bug. No one would have thought that was going to be as bad as it got. It destroyed everything. All of you know this. This year alone it was predicted that sixty percent of the crops would be lost if we didn't do anything. The Secretary of Agriculture called me," Art said. "Find a solution. Nothing was working on them. Nothing previously tried. The pred bug was impervious to anything and they multiplied at an astronomical rate."

Craig spoke, "I read an article that if they weren't eliminated this year, they'd be everywhere."

"One shouldn't mess with mother nature," Art said. "That's correct. So I was called in to find a solution. And it hit one night in a hotel when I saw a bed bug. *Beauveria Bassiana*. A fungus. The hardest bug to kill is a bed bug. They're resilient. Yet, they die from *Beauveria Bassiana*. So I needed to find the right fungus. It's not unusual or uncommon to use fungi or bacteria on bugs to wipe them out. But nothing worked. I had to create a superior fungus. One that didn't hurt plants or agriculture, only the pred bugs. I mean I knew we could lose other bugs, maybe some birds, but the end result was the elimination of the pred bug and that was most important. All testing showed it was safe."

"When did you learn it wasn't?" Kit asked.

"A week before the extermination blitzkrieg launch. The whole plan was to spray everywhere within a twenty-four-hour window, all across the globe. Now you can't spray every location so you have to rely on using a highly concentrated formula that would carry with the wind, jet streams, a global extermination. The effort was quite ambitious. Because the spores lose effectiveness in twenty-four hours, they would spot exterminate after that."

"So that," Kit said, "was how you determined which places were safe."

Bill answered, "Yes, but it was a crap shoot. There are a few places that were clear, safe places. Griffin was one. There aren't many."

Art added, "If we'd just had more time. We tried to warn them but no one listened. Testing never went beyond the four-hour mark with humans, twenty-four hours with mice. It was so rushed."

Kit shook his head in confusion. "I don't understand. How can you not test longer?"

"There was nothing that indicated long-term effects. We were worried about the immediate effects since the bugs died instantly," Art answered.

"Four hours is not long term," said Cass.

"No, it's not. My colleague discovered the mice were dying at the twenty-five-hour mark. They showed no symptoms whatsoever. It was by accident that we learned what it did to people. The tech that removed the live mouse, she didn't have gloves on. The spores of the fungus transferred to her skin. It spread, the skin deteriorated, there was no way to stop it. We tried but she died in twelve hours. And that was when we learned. The fungus was releasing extremely high levels of mycotoxins. Which meant each mode of infection or affection caused different symptoms. Much like anthrax."

Craig commented, "Cutaneous, inhalation, and gastrointestinal. Eat, touch, breathe."

"Exactly," Art said. "Sometimes all three. The symptoms would be horrendous. If they caught it by the skin exposure, a rash would just eat the skin, releasing the same deadly toxin into the blood stream until death. Inhalation or ingestion would be a faster, less painful death. But we don't know. Because we were never able to see its effects beyond the tech. All our warnings were based on her and for that, we were dismissed."

"So you ran," Kit said.

"My team did," Art replied. "I thought they'd be here."

Kit paced some, then stopped with a swing of his hand. "Do we know though? Do we know it caused this effect? I mean what you are saying is the extermination carried out across the globe wiped everyone out except for a few places. Do we know this to be true? We are in Griffin, the out-of-touch capital of the world."

Cass peered up to him. "You tried Seaver. No luck."

"Then I'll go there." Kit walked toward the door.

"Officer, stop," Art called out. "I beg of you not to. It hasn't hit the twenty-four-hour mark. It takes at least twenty-four hours for the spores to die off, lose effectiveness. I know that. You go there; it could still be there. Wait. Wait until tomorrow and go. In the meantime, we need to go door to door. Check to see who was in town, who was not and if anyone has any symptoms. Our main goal is to give the fungus no more hosts to latch on to."

"So contact tracing," Craig said. "What do we do with those infected? If we find any."

"Isolate. One area," Art replied. "Make them as comfortable as possible. Twenty-four hours, spore free, we are in the clear."

"What do we tell people?" Kit asked. "Just knock on the door and say hey, we need to check you in case you are going to die?"

Art shook his head. "Tell them the truth. Well, in part. Tell them there is a biological threat, you're checking on anyone who may have left town and ask if they are experiencing any symptoms. After the town is in the clear, then we tell them. We tell them the truth when we know the extent of everything."

"I don't think you'll find anyone," Cass said. "No one really leaves. We're not a big social town."

"That's optimistic and good to hear," Art said. "The sooner we get on this the better. Officer, I need you to make sure no one leaves town."

"I have two off-duty officers I'll call in," Kit replied.

Craig exhaled loudly, stood, and slowly shook his head. "I never thought it was possible. But we're looking at complete omnicide."

Art nodded his agreement. "Yes, because if I am right. This is global."

Cass looked left to right, Art to Craig. "Wait. What? Stop. Omnicide? What the hell is that?"

Craig explained, "It starts with good intentions. Something that is to protect and better the world. Basically, it's something man made that causes the extinction of the human race. Obviously, it has never happened. Yet, that's what we have. If he is right, if this hit everywhere, it's a pure definition of the word," Craig said. "Omnicide."

13.
HIDE AND SEEK

It had only been an hour, but it finally hit Cass that her friend was gone. Brian was dead.

She had to tell Walt, or would he just find out?

Without a doubt, she wanted Eb to hear it from her and since he had agreed to be part of Lena's show, she made her way back out to Ada's, bringing Art with her, just to check him.

Even though she was certain that Eb hadn't left town or had any contact with Brian, she wanted to be sure.

While Art talked to him, ran that light over him, Cass stared out the kitchen window. She watched them filming the garden portion of Lena's show.

Had she not known it was Ada, Cass wouldn't have recognized her. Her hair was done and her makeup was natural looking and perfect.

She stood at the window, arms folded staring out for a while.

"Clear," Art announced as they returned to the kitchen.

"Told you," Eb said. "I didn't leave or speak to anyone other than you, Cass. You okay?" He stepped to her.

"I'll be fine. This is just a lot right now," Cass said. She looked back out the window, saw they were gone and within a few seconds, the back door opened.

"Back again?" Ada asked. "Who's your friend?"

Before Cass could answer, Lena smiled brightly. "Oh! Are you here for lunch? I made a lovely quiche and salad."

Cass shifted her eyes back and forth from Ada to Eb.

"You don't like quiche?" Lena asked.

"That's not it," Ada answered for Cass. "Something is going on. Spill it. Who's the guy?"

"I'm Art Bohr," Art introduced himself. "I'm a scientist."

"Ada," Cass said gently, "I know this is going to sound ridiculous and hard to believe, we're all still processing it. But it seems the global extermination of the pred bugs, may just be a global extermination of the human race."

Silence.

"Wow," Art said. "That was simplified and blunt."

Kat started to laugh. "She's joking." He paused and the smile dropped from his young face. "She's not."

Cass shook her head.

Almost as if she were expecting it, Ada walked to the fridge. "So, basically the super 'kill off the bug' stuff isn't so safe for humans. I could have told them that." She opened the fridge. "Iced tea, anyone?" She pulled out the pitcher. "Art, you have something to do with this?"

"I was on the team that invented the fungus that was meant to eradicate the pred bugs."

"And you didn't know it wasn't safe."

"Not at first," Art replied. "By the time we figured it out, they wouldn't stop. They said our data wasn't strong enough. That the impact on human life was mild compared to what the pred bugs would do."

"I take it they didn't think about global extermination," Ada said.

Art shook his head.

"So why are you in Griffin?" Ada asked. "Last town to try to save?"

"Last town alive."

The pitcher nearly toppled from Ada's hand at the same time as Lena gasped.

"There could be a few other places that weren't affected with the drop. Places like Griffin, blips on a map that fell through the cracks of the wind patterns and jet streams that carried the fungus."

"A fungus." Ada nodded. "How much do you know about how it affects humans?"

"Not much. We barely started our research when the drop happened. I know it infects three ways. Skin, lungs, ingestion."

"Like anthrax," Ada said, "and I'm betting, like anthrax, it's a death sentence if you ingest it."

Art lowered his head and looked at her through the tops of his eyes. "It's a death sentence if the spores attach to you."

"Nonsense." Ada shook her head.

"Once it's in the blood stream…"

"How long does it take to get into the blood stream from the skin?"

"I…I don't know," Art stuttered.

"Find out."

"It's not that easy," Art said.

"Yes, it is, find someone with the rash."

"The spores die off at twenty-four hours, so does the person, it happens rather fast."

"You're telling me," Ada said, "that a person gets a rash from this and is dead in twenty-four hours?"

"Yes."

Ada scoffed.

Eb spoke gently, "Ada, why are you having a hard time believing this?"

"Because I know how his stuff works. I was a nurse for many years. I also know nature very well and this is impossible."

"That's because," Lena interjected, "this isn't all nature. He made this or manipulated it so it's also man made."

"We came, Ada," Cass said, "to let you know and we're checking to see if anyone left town, or was outside of Griffin, after eleven in the morning yesterday."

"I wasn't," Ada replied. "None of us were."

"Brian was," Cass said solemnly. "Patty and Mrs. Sanders."

Ada looked at Cass curiously.

"Brian and Patty are dead. Kit is checking Mrs. Sanders," Cass said.

"Oh, honey I'm sorry." Ada then looked at Art. "Did you bring stuff to work on this?"

"I did."

"Can't you get a sample from Brian?" Ada asked. "Work with that."

"I can. But the spores are probably dead by now—they can only spread while they're alive," Art explained.

"Does that reset the clock?" Ada asked.

Art nodded. "Yes, so Griffin won't be risk free until everyone who has it has passed and the spores are inactive on any surface they happened to be upon. Griffin didn't get hit with the agent, so any fungus or spores were brought in by outside sources or were passed on by an infected person."

"And I take it you're doing contact tracing?" Ada asked.

"The town doctor and I, along with the police force, are," Art replied.

"It should be easy," Cass spoke hopefully. "I mean, Brian stayed home and we checked the two places he was. They were clean. Mrs. Sanders had the rash cream delivered, she never left the house, and the pharmacy man just put it on her porch. So we think we have this."

Ada shook her head. "You're forgetting about Patty. Brian's wife does nails. Her shop was open until seven last night. Lord knows how many hands she touched."

"Shit," Cass said.

"Will you…" Lena nervously spoke. "Will you excuse me. I'm going to use the land line and try John again. If that doesn't work I will try every number in my phone. This can't be everywhere. It can't be in the big cities. It just sounds so impossible. We would have heard. Excuse me." She hurried out of the room.

Eb exhaled with a slight whistle as he sat down. "Obviously it hasn't sunk in she's in Griffin, and we run two days behind with the news." He shifted his eyes to Cass. "No offense."

"None taken."

Art faced her. "Cass, can you take me to this nail shop? Maybe we can go inside and look at the appointment book. See who all came to see her and go from there."

"And do what? Quarantine and try to help them?" Ada asked.

"Yes," Art said, impassioned. "That's the plan, and look for others and quarantine them."

"How about this?" Ada suggested. "You need to get a good twenty-four hours for these spores to lose effectiveness. Meaning, you need to cut them off from a host. Instead of searching for anyone who has a rash, why don't you just tell everyone they can't leave where they are, at this moment, for twenty-four hours. If they're at the store, give them a chance to go home, but home they stay for twenty-four hours. After that, no one has contact with anyone else, it's done. And since that shit was dropped yesterday. It's done everywhere else."

"Threat over?" Cass asked Art.

"Go into a lockdown, yeah. Yeah, it couldn't hurt."

"All well and fine," Eb said, "you wanna say we're safe. What then? You're saying the rest of the world or almost all the world is dead? Are we sure? I mean, we're Griffin, we're cut off. We wouldn't know one way or another. No cable, no news, no internet, no cells. How did we know? We may be the isolated case."

"That's easy," Kat, who had been quiet, spoke up. "We wait the twenty-four hours and we go find out."

Out of the mind and mouth of the youth came a logical suggestion. Go out and see. The thing was, Cass wasn't sure she wanted to know. Because to her, those in Griffin were what mattered and if the buck stopped at Griffin, it wasn't going to be all that different to her.

<><><><>

For as long as Kit could remember the position of mayor of Griffin was always held by a Wilson. Mark being the latest Wilson to carry that honor. All of them were homegrown and had Griffin's best interest at heart. Although, there really wasn't much 'politically' that needed to be done, nor was there ever a crisis...until that moment.

Kit hated to do it, he hated to call Mark, but he had to. There was a chance Mark wouldn't believe it, and Kit would have to take him to Brian's to show him the body, but Mark was calm and rational, only asking, "Are we sure it's everywhere?"

113

"No." That's all Kit could say. He was curious himself. He went on the computer, typed in a news site, and allowed the page to load.

When he left to meet Mark at Mrs. Sanders' home, it had barely made it to three percent loaded.

Kit went in alone, while Mark stayed outside. He wore a face mask and gloves, and carried a pocket black light.

He hoped it wouldn't come to that. But when Mrs. Sanders didn't open the door, Kit went in.

It was the same feel; the smell was a little worse, but like Brian and Patty, Mrs. Sanders had passed. She bore the bleeding rash on her face and legs. Only difference between her and Brian was that she had died in her reclining chair, feet propped up, a can of soda next to her. Brian had been on the floor, looking as if he'd tried desperately to crawl for help.

He ran the black light over her. He jumped nearly a foot in the air when the ringing telephone broke the silence.

He looked to his left and to the older phone.

It rang and rang.

Finally, Kit walked over and answered it. He would just say Mrs. Sanders wasn't available. That wasn't lying. "Hello, Sanders Residence, Officer Modine, Griffin PD speaking."

"Oh, Kit," Cass said. "I'm glad I caught you."

"Cass…Cass, what are you doing calling Mrs. Sanders' house?"

"I can't reach your cell phone. I've been trying for fifteen minutes to reach you there. No one answered."

"She's not gonna answer, Cass. Is there an emergency?"

"No, but we have an idea and we need to talk to you immediately."

Kit reluctantly agreed to listen but only for a minute, then he hung up and left the house.

Mark was outside waiting. He leaned against the squad car. Not his own which was parked directly in front of the police car. He was average in height, but thicker, or as Cass called him 'jolly' with a bald head, still sporting the grandpa hair on the sides.

He liked Mark Wilson. He was a good guy and Kit never had any problems with him professionally or personally. Although Mark was ten years older so Kit really never got to know him well until he became mayor…and Cass' husband.

"Well?" Mark asked.

Kit shook his head. "She's gone."

"What about this fungus?"

"I honestly didn't see it, but that could be me. I'm no expert," Kit replied.

"What do we do?" Mark asked.

"Art said not to touch the body for twenty-four hours, then I suppose we can call Fillman's and have them come and get her. Brian and Patty too."

"And just bury them like nothing happened?"

"Yeah, I suppose. I mean, these are our people, Mark. This town is small enough to do that. Fillman's has been taking care of that since before our time."

"Jesus, Kit." Mark shook his head. "Are we sure? I mean, I am not questioning these deaths. I mean this crisis. This is Griffin. "

"And we're all thinking the same thing," Kit said. "We don't know. Just because we can't hear or read anything doesn't mean that's all gone. Hell, remember last October when we were down for four days?"

Mark released a fast, sharp breath. "Yeah, everyone was convinced there was some sort of alien invasion. No one wanted to leave town to find out."

"No one did."

"You wanted to," Mark said.

"And you wouldn't allow it. Even though you knew it wasn't real and it drove me nuts."

"Yes," Mark said. "However, it was the most excitement we had in a while."

"Where in the hell did that come from anyhow?"

"The damn *Times*. Cass and her stories. I mean, yes, it was just a 'what if' piece, but still, sent everyone into a frenzy."

"I don't think this is the same thing," Kit said. "And I will go out and see."

Mark nodded. "We're gonna have to. We have physical proof that something is happening and a scientist claiming it's the end of the world."

"Two nights ago, Brad got in that accident," Kit said. "Cass and Brian along with Eb said a sick deer went nuts and caused it."

"But that was before the massive extermination attempt."

"It was, but the government has been dropping in small doses and areas the last three days. Harrison's Nectarine farm got sprayed Sunday afternoon."

"How do you know?"

"County called, said they were blocking off Miller Run Road sixteen miles up."

"So that would make sense with the deer."

"Could," Kit said. "Small amounts—probably a kill radius a lot smaller than we're dealing with now. And before you ask, I tried to call Harrison. Nothing."

"Damn it." Mark paced a few circles and then grabbed a pack of cigarettes from his pocket and lit one. "Where is our scientist now?"

"With Cass at Ada's."

"His father, the man that came with him?"

"At the motel. They're gonna set up a few rooms for testing and patients if we have anyone. Listen, Cass called."

Immediately and excitedly, Mark grabbed for his cell phone. "Are the phones working?"

Kit cringed. "No, she called me in there."

"What in Christ name is wrong with that woman? I get it she needed to reach you, but goddamn, get in the truck and drive to you. What did she want?"

"Her, Ada, and this scientist think we should go into a lockdown. Stay at home. Twenty-four hours. By then the danger will have passed. Tell folks there is a county medical crisis, to report any symptoms to the police department. Do not leave, help will come to them. And to shelter where they are for twenty-four hours. Give them an opportunity to go home, or stay put."

"Well, that does make sense. I guess. Easier to drive around making that announcement over and over than go door to door, right?"

"Exactly."

Mark reached out and gave a swat to Kit's arm. "I'll man the phones at the station, while you do just that."

"What? Ride around using the PA to make the announcement?"

"That's the only way. Check in with me," Mark said. "I'm sure the radio works." Mark walked to his own car.

"Hey, Mark, don't you think as Mayor, you ought to be the one doing this?"

Mark opened his driver's door. "People like me, Kit. I doubt they'll even notice they have to stay in if I do it. If they're gonna get angry about the order, I'd rather have you do it, since they already have a stick up their ass about you," he said with a smile, just as he got in his own car.

Kit was dumbfounded. Mark was joking. People liked Kit, he thought. But he didn't know for sure. No one in Griffin really said much or complained. That was a good thing, because he truly didn't expect them to say much or complain about the lockdown either. Typically, they'd just brush it off as lack of communication with the outside world. Kit believed they'd handle it. He hoped, because he didn't want a repeat of last October and the ridiculous alien invasion drama.

<><><><>

Bill wasn't a science guy. He left that up to his son and Bill was proud, but he knew Art was down on himself, and just wanted to conquer the thing he'd created.

It was a beast.

One didn't have to be a scientist to know that.

Most spores on fungi fall off and die within minutes; the spores on Art's fungus lived a day. Long enough to find a new host.

Art had made the hotel into his own research center and clinic. The owner wasn't too agreeable at first until the police made the rounds announcing the emergency. Then the owner offered whatever was needed.

It was getting late; Bill had tried unsuccessfully to get a signal. He wanted to get in the car and drive until he got one, but it wasn't safe, so he paced a lot around that motel parking lot, looking at his watch, as Art went in and out of rooms to treat those seven people that had been infected by Patty the nail technician. He didn't venture far from the office because Bill was on phone duty. Ada was calling constantly with suggestions.

She even dropped off a concoction that stunk to high heaven. Bill chuckled when he remembered Art getting frustrated with her.

"I appreciate it," Art said.

"Soak cotton and place it on the wound, soak it."

Art smiled politely. "Ada, honestly, we're not talking nature where the frontier way can kick its butt. This is a manipulated fungus. I think only science can beat it."

"Give the frontiers way a shot. I'll be back with more things to try."

Time was of the essence. Art could only guess how long it took to get into the blood stream and all the patients had been infected by way of skin. He and Dr. Craig were working overtime trying things. Everything.

After grabbing a beer from the motel owner's fridge, Bill spotted Art coming out of room nine, making his way to room twelve, where he had a lab set up.

"Art, hold up," Bill hollered and made his way over.

"Hey, Dad."

"Take a break."

"I can't. I will, but not right now."

"How is everything?"

"Well, number nine doesn't seem to be progressing. I have a skin culture I want to look at. I think we may have paused it. If that's the case, we just need to figure out how to stop it and cure it."

"Stinky tincture?" Bill asked.

"Yeah, how about that?"

"Ada is the type of woman who won't let you live that down."

"Don't I know it," Art said. "Maybe she has viable ideas for stopping this all together. You know she never got the pred bugs."

119

"Really? That's amazing. Art, I understand you wanting to help these women if you can. But after their fates are sealed, it's over, right?"

Art hesitated in answering. "I don't know, Dad. The spores need a living host. Fungi continuously adapt and mutate. I know from testing previously it does not attach to plants or grass."

"If it kills everything it attaches to, it has to die out. Right?"

"I would think. I am not going to say for sure, though, because there may be something out there that can be a carrier and spread this thing all over again. For that," Art said, "I just want to be ready."

<><><><>

"Son of a gun," Kit cursed out loud, staring at the computer in the police station. "Thirty-eight percent? Things loaded faster in 1995." He tossed a pencil and sat back. He was bored, but at least the phone had stopped ringing.

The questions were driving him nuts.

"If I have an open wound will I get it?"

"Only if you're exposed."

"I was in Seaver last week…"

"Can I just hang out all night at Brass Balls and Beers?"

He had been going all day with it. They'd discovered seven people, all women that had developed symptoms. All clients of Patty's. He and Officer Floyd were the only two officers left in town. The chief never returned, and the other officer happened to be in Flagstaff.

Floyd took two men up to Miller Run Road. They were on deer patrol. Kit was fearful the deer could make their way into town, and they had to be eliminated before that happened.

120

It was crazy.

He did laugh when he thought back to earlier in the day when he started driving around making the announcement. Kit was less than enthusiastic.

"This is a county health emergency. You are advised to stay in your home for the next twenty-four hours and avoid all contact."

He passed Cass just outside Brass Balls and Beers and she waved him down.

"You're not really getting through," she said. "No one is even listening to you."

"I'm doing what I can. You have a better idea, by all means." He showed her the microphone.

"Oh, really?" she asked excitedly. "Can I?"

"Be my guest."

Cass got in the car.

"Attention Griffin, there is an airborne contagion sweeping across the nation. Stay inside. Stay alive. Report any suspicious symptoms to the Griffin Police Station. You'll be informed what do to. Stay inside."

She had a tone of dramatic seriousness to her. Kit didn't think that would work either until he returned the station and the phone rang off the hook.

Now it was quiet. He supposed everyone was sleeping or getting close to it.

The dangling bell above the door jingled and Kit looked up. "You're supposed to stay home."

"Oh, please, I haven't been home all day," Cass said, walking into the station. "I've been at Brass Balls and Beers answering the calls."

"People are calling there?" Kit asked.

"Oh sure, they knew I was there. Anyhow, between that and Ada digging plants and herbs, mixing strange concoctions for Art, I've been busy."

"Anything working?"

"I don't know. I do know Mary Wentworth and Cleo Smith are bad. Worse than the others."

"That's sad to know. Why are you here?"

"Go home."

"What?"

"Go home, Kit, your son is there waiting on his dinner and his father. He's scared. He doesn't say it, but he is. Go home."

"I would love to be with my son. I can't leave the station."

"You leave it every night."

"Yeah," Kit said. "But I turn it over to county. County is not answering. We should have an official member of the force in here."

"Floyd?" Cass asked.

"He's stopping any infected deer."

"So, okay. Make me a deputy."

Kit laughed.

"I'm serious."

"Cass, only the chief can do that and it needs to be signed by the mayor. The chief isn't coming back. I think we know that."

"So does that mean my restraining order is now null and void?"

"Oh, Cass, stop."

"Kit you need to go home."

Kit sighed out, rocked a few times in his chair, and stood. "Fine." He went back to the chief's office and returned handing a badge to Cass. "You're hereby deputized. I'll get Mark to make it official in the morning."

"Do I get a gun?"

"No!" Kit snapped.

"Can I carry my own?"

"You don't need a gun to monitor the station."

"Yeah, but we're the one live spot in the world. A bright light in a dark world."

"Christ, Cass, so dramatic."

"I'm serious," Cass said. "What if surviving marauders come in here with their lawlessness and…"

Kit tossed her keys. "Only if that happens. You can hit the armory room in the back."

"So you're going home?"

"Yes, thank you. And do me a favor, sit behind my desk. I'm waiting on a webpage to load."

Cass walked over to his computer. "Sports again?"

"No. The news." Kit headed toward the door. "Call me if there are any problems. Thank you, Cass. I mean it."

"You're welcome, and Kit? Relax some okay. Play a game with Kat. Get some rest. Tomorrow is a big day."

"Yeah, I know and I am not looking forward to it. I'm trying not to think about it. Tomorrow we find out if we really are the only bright light left in this world. I honestly…" Kit tapped the door. "I'm scared to find out."

With a ding of the bell, Kit was gone before Cass could say, "Me too." She sat back in his chair, thinking about the next day, watching that progress bar hold steady at thirty-nine percent, and praying constantly in her mind that they were only out of touch and that communication was down, that the rest of the world was still just as bright as Griffin. Inwardly, Cass knew that probably wasn't the case.

14.
NOTHING VENTURED

May 7

The police station was quiet, all that needed to be had been said in the moments after Kit left.

Cass argued she didn't think he should go alone, but his rebuttal had merit. If indeed it ended up being dangerous then only one person in Griffin would be affected.

Art was there, waiting to find out, as was Mark.

Kit asked Art, "Are you sure? Are you really sure it's safe? We're sending him to Seaver."

"He's going on his own. That was his decision and you know that," Art said. "And it's safe. I'd bet my life on it. I know the spores die off."

Art didn't stay long, he had work to do and he and Craig still had two patients holding on.

Oddly, Lena was there. She was using the land lines and fax. She had Ada making calls as well. She'd come up with a plan. Cass thought it was a good one. She had enough people in her phone's contacts—business acquaintances, friends, publicists, chefs, and even fans. They spanned the globe. Some she didn't even know. That didn't matter, there were enough that someone out there somewhere would answer.

She wrote down numbers for Ada, then took her phone to the station.

Cass watched her. Lena didn't look like the same woman she'd met two days earlier. Her hair was in a ponytail, she didn't wear makeup. Not that she needed it, she was naturally beautiful, but it wasn't the Lena she projected to everyone.

She tucked a falling strand of hair behind her ear and picked up the phone again. She looked at her cell, then dialed the number.

It was the same routine. Lift, look, dial, listen...hang up.

With each failed attempt her face grew more drawn. Cass knew the reason behind Lena's diligence to reach someone. It wasn't to see if the world was alive, it was for hope that her children were alive. Lena hadn't said it, Cass didn't need her to. She knew all too well that desperate, devastated look and burden that Lena carried.

No one told her to give up. Cass certainly wouldn't. She supposed she wanted to find that hope as well.

A hiss of static caused everyone to jump. It was followed by Kit's voice.

"Griffin, this is Modine."

His voice was a little distorted and soft.

Mark dove for the radio. "We can barely hear you," Mark said. "You must be close."

There as a pause, then static. "Three miles. I'll radio when I can."

"Be careful."

"Roger that," Kit said. "Out."

Mark held on to the radio for a few moments, then set it down and slowly turned around. "He's almost in Seaver."

"We heard," Cass replied. "And...we'll know soon enough."

"Yep," Mark said. "We'll know if anyone else is out there."

"God." Cass closed her eyes. "Let's hope."

Her eyes immediately popped wide open and she spun in her chair when Lena shrieked out excitedly.

"Oh my God." Lena stood up. "This is Lena Feeny. Is that really you, Trixie?"

Cass was in shock, and hopeful...Lena had reached someone. Now all they needed to know was where.

Seaver, AZ

Anxiety swelled within his being the second he saw Hillbilly Jim's truck. Things were just worse when he saw the birds, each of them showing signs of being infected by the fungus.

Where was everyone? Had they all gotten so sick, that they went back to their homes?

More than likely that was the case.

He thought of those in Griffin, the women who innocently had their nails done only to be contaminated by Patty.

The rash began on the hands of each of them. The ones with more complicated nails had it the worst. It spread from there. Some of Ada's tinctures slowed down the progress, but whether it was too late when they found them or not, bottom line...the tinctures only slowed down the inevitable death.

His first thought was to radio, but he knew he needed some answers. He wanted more than anything to find out why everyone just left. That wasn't the case. They hadn't left at all.

In a deep loud, booming voice, he called out, "Anyone there? Is anyone in Seaver? Hello!"

He walked slowly down the street avoiding the bird carcasses, stopping in front of the police station.

Hating to do it, and fearful of what he would see, he walked in.

Immediately the smell of death and decomposition hit him. His paper mask did nothing to block it. He brought the back of his hand under his nose and turned his head with a wince. When he did that he cringed, thinking, *Son of a bitch, I touched that door handle.* And he recalled Art telling him not to touch his face. He hoped if anything was on his gloved hand, it didn't slip through the fibers of the mask.

But that cringe and wince brought him an answer, the fate and whereabouts of the Chief of Police of Griffin.

Kit didn't see him at first when he walked in, but there he was on his side, lying on the reception area couch. His arm dangled, clutching a blood-stained wastepaper basket next to him. Kit turned and didn't have to walk far to see not only the sheriff, but two other Seaver officers. All at their desks, heads down, each with a phone to their ear.

Kit could only imagine they were trying desperately to call for help.

He didn't need to see the others to know that Seaver was dead.

Perhaps he would drive through town, using the PA just to call in case someone had beaten it.

He left the police station and saw him as soon as he stepped outside.

The sight of the man standing across the street caused a stir in Kit. The man wasn't from Seaver, or at least Kit didn't think so. He wore a biohazard suit, but he wore it without the hood or gloves. He carried a case in one hand, in the other a duffle bag.

"I heard you calling," he said with a British accent. "It's fine. You don't need the mask. The spores and fungus are inactive."

"How do you know?" Kit asked.

"I checked. I have been here since early this morning. It's been long enough." He stepped to Kit. "Niles Proctor."

"Kit Modine. So...where is everyone?" Kit asked. "Have you looked?"

"Yes, in their homes or the Urgent Care. You name a place in town, you'll find them. No survivors, despite them trying."

"Do you think they know what happened?" Kit asked.

"Without a doubt. About two hours after the blanket extermination, authorities were urging people to get inside, stay inside, seal up for a day. But...they had already been exposed. From what I could tell, it entered the blood stream within minutes and their fate was sealed."

"How did you survive?" Kit asked.

Niles ran his hand down his suit. "I was in a sealed lab and wore this when out for the first thirty-six hours. I knew it was coming. Our team all divided up, trying to get to safe areas. I didn't want to run, not without seeing if there was some way I could help."

"Did you?"

"In a way. I found something in the restaurant." He raised the duffle bag. "Seems some sort of camera crew was in town. The camera was actually out and in the hand of one of the men. It's broken, but I'm sure we can retrieve footage from the hard drive or insert drive. Whoever it was filmed the last days of Seaver."

Kit exhaled heavily, there was something about hearing those words that saddened him even more. "Where are you headed now?"

"My final destination. This was my last stop."

"And where would that be?" Kit asked.

"Griffin."

Kit only nodded once. Somehow, hearing that from Niles didn't surprise him at all.

Los Angeles, CA

Trixie Powers for the most part led a life of leisure. She'd skyrocketed to fame after a sex video of her and a famous rock star leaked online. It wasn't her doing, but she was glad. One four-minute video of shame for a life of fame was worth it.

Her social media profiles had a combined following of close to twenty million people, which really was nothing compared to a lot of people she knew and was friends with.

When she had returned from a night of partying, she'd staggered into her bedroom holding a just opened bottle of champagne. She'd given strict instructions that she didn't want to be disturbed and to let her sleep until she woke up; a message for the cleaning lady who came in on Mondays to leave her room be, and one for her personal assistant who seemed to always be annoyingly opening her blinds at eight a.m.

She'd had a hard night. Arguing with a friend and being seen by the paparazzi. She had to defend her actions on social media, then immediately issue an apology for being insensitive.

She was worn out.

Before going to bed, she grabbed a bottle of water from the little fridge in her bedroom minibar, placed it on her nightstand with three ibuprofen, and then after chugging some champagne, she fell asleep.

When Trixie woke, she did as she always did: sat up, swiped up the ibuprofen and water, then lifted her phone as she swallowed the pills.

She first noticed the time of two p.m., but the alert of the message from Anita, her assistant, caught her attention.

"DO NOT LEAVE THE ROOM OR HOUSE." It said more, but she had to unlock it to read the whole thing. Clearly it was some sort of joke, Trixie thought. Then she read the message.

"DO NOT LEAVE THE ROOM OR HOUSE. The mass pred bug extermination went bad. It's killing people. Do not leave your room until you know it's safe."

Immediately, she replied, "Where are you?"

"Home," came the reply.

"Is this for real?" asked Trixie.

"Yes," replied Anita. "The news is still on for now. They just issued the warning. Before I left your house, I put a towel under the sill of your door. Stay safe."

"What about you?"

"I'm already exposed."

Trixie had no idea what that meant or how serious it was. While firing up the browser on her phone, she grabbed the remote and put on the television.

"Right now we still have power," the female newscaster said. "How long it will remain, we don't know. Right now, again, if you are just joining us, the one-hour safety window was wrong. If you have not left your home, you are advised to stay inside, seal all doors and windows, and do not leave. If you are experiencing any of the following symptoms…"

Trixie increasingly panicked with every symptom the newscaster gave. Even though coffee was an option in her room, she grabbed the warm champagne and drank.

That newscast was now two days ago. It had gone off the air just after midnight the first day. The cameras kept running, showing an empty news desk and eventually even the cameras went down.

Trixie still had power, that was a good thing.

She didn't leave. She had food and water in her room, but with her home set far back on her property she couldn't see the street or know what was going on outside.

She'd spent the two days trying to get answers, reaching people, and had nearly given up until Lena called.

She wasn't the last one left. Not by a long shot.

Griffin, AZ

When death came for the woman in room nine, it was rapid and vicious. Art also believed treating her and being unable to save her was inhumane. It prolonged her suffering and her family's pain as they watched her leave this world.

He covered her and then called Fillman's funeral home to tell them he had the last of them. Fillman's could retrieve the body another day.

That was it.

Room nine's passing marked the end of the fungus in Griffin, or so Art believed.

Had he failed the woman? After all, he wasn't a medical doctor. He was a scientist, one far removed from treating people.

Maybe if someone far more experienced had been there. Then again, not even Dr. Craig could do anything.

131

It was hopeless.

After showering, Art grabbed a soda from the vending machine and walked toward town. They'd be hearing from Kit soon. Last he checked in, Kit had arrived in Seaver and no further word was given.

It was safe for Kit to be there. Art was a hundred percent certain; he knew the spores.

It was strange for him when he walked down the street, hearing the noise coming from the car shop. Life wasn't stopping in Griffin. When the twenty-four hours were up, people had gone back to work.

Back to life as usual.

If Kit came back with the news that Seaver was a dead horse, then life would not be normal again. At least not for Art. Maybe the people in Griffin were different.

He was starting to believe that when he heard the shop, saw people coming out of the coffee shop, going into the diner, and two men sat outside the barber shop.

They hadn't any clue, Art thought. None whatsoever or they didn't care.

Perhaps they didn't realize or know ten people in their little town had died.

He'd ask Cass. He saw her pacing back and forth outside the police station.

"Hey," Art called out when he approached her.

She turned around. "Hey."

"Waiting on Kit, I suppose."

"Yeah, he radioed he's on his way back."

"Did he say anything?" Art asked.

"Nope. Left me hanging. It's like waiting on the season premiere of a show to find out what happened."

Art smiled and his eyes caught the badge on her belt buckle. "So, a badge?"

"I'm a deputy now. It was official this morning."

"Wow, congratulations."

"Thanks."

"Can I ask you something?"

"Shoot."

"Things seem normal. I mean the barber shop is open. Eb is in his shop."

"They're still setting up for the festival too," Cass said. "Did you see that?'

"No, I didn't. Which makes it even stranger. Do they not care about what's going on?"

"They...they don't know really what's going on. Well, Eb does. No one else. We told them only what we announced," Cass said. "So to them, they beat the mark and are okay."

"They don't know about their fellow townspeople dying. It was almost five percent of your population."

"They don't know. They will," Cass replied. "Mark, our mayor, will talk to everyone tonight and Walt is running a special edition of the paper. I wrote three obituaries this morning."

"And you probably want to get answers about Seaver."

"Absolutely," Cass said. "We're not giving up. I'm not. If Seaver isn't alright, then we'll try somewhere else."

"You can be sure if Seaver is down then everywhere else is, too."

"No." Cass shook her head. "We know for a fact..." Her attention was drawn from her thoughts and to the police car that pulled up.

Another car was behind him.

"He found someone," Cass said in surprise.

"No, that man isn't from Seaver." Art quickly walked toward the other car. "That man is a colleague of mine."

Cass started to say "what?" but Kit stepped from the police car. "Well?" Cass asked.

Kit shook his head. "All gone."

Cass closed her eyes. "Oh my God."

"Lena's camera crew was filming. We can see what happened at the end. I mean, that's something."

"It is," Cass said. "Here's something else. Good news."

"Please. Tell me."

"Lena made contact."

"What?"

Immediately Art and Niles echoed the shock

"What?" Art asked. "Contact."

"On the phone," Cass said. "Los Angeles. So you see, Art, we have to keep looking. If someone is alive there, they could be alive anywhere."

15.
SOUGHT AND REFUGE

Mark wore a white button-down dress shirt, no tie. He looked ready for a day at the office. He paced a little in the station, arms folded, as he listened to Kit. Then he went silent, doing some sort of thinking face before he spoke. "I am going to agree with Cass," he said. "We need to go out there. Search. Look for people. Create teams. They aren't just gonna come to us. Those who survived need to stick together. As long as there is no threat to the teams we send out."

Niles shook his head. "None that I can see or saw. They do need to be prepared in case they run into less than stellar survivors."

"I want to go with Crazy Ada," said Cass.

"What?" Kit snapped. "She's needed here."

Before an argument could ensue, Lena brightly called out, "I have her. I have her on the phone."

Mark snapped his finger. "Put her on the speaker phone."

Lena just stared at the phone. "How?"

With a slight grumble, Mark walked over and pressed the button, placing down the receiver. "Trixie? Are you there?"

"I am."

"How are you?" Mark asked.

"Scared."

"That's to be expected."

"Trixie, this is Doctor Niles Proctor. Tell me, are you experiencing any symptoms? Rash, trouble breathing, stomach issues?"

"No. None. I'm physically fine."

"Good," Niles said.

Art spoke up. "What are you seeing there, Trixie, in LA?"

"Nothing really. My house is pretty set back from the road."

"Have you left your house at all?" Art asked.

"I haven't left my room."

"Not once?" asked Art.

"No, I have everything I need here," Trixie said. "And the news said to stay put."

Art looked at Niles. "Did you know the news was broadcasting?"

Niles nodded. "Yes, but not for long. We also don't know how long communication and power will be up. Trixie? You can leave the house. It is perfectly safe."

"Are you sure?" she asked.

"Yes," answered Art. "You should leave. Pack what you need, bring supplies, and make your way here. It won't take you more than seven hours. I would suggest leaving first thing tomorrow morning. We'll give you directions because we don't know how long things will be up so don't rely on GPS."

"I don't want to be alone," Trixie said. "I mean no one does. But no one knows it's safe, they're scared to leave their homes or apartments. No one has even answered so they'll be glad to hear."

Kit looked at Cass curiously. "Trixie, this is Officer Modine. Who will be glad to hear that it's safe?"

"Everyone waiting inside," Trixie replied.

"Okay, so you're not meaning specific people," Kit said. "You're speaking in general."

"I don't know their names. I know their usernames."

A huge 'what' of shock rang out around the room.

"Usernames?" Kit asked. "As in social media?"

"Yes," Trixie answered. "I mean I have millions of followers, nothing compared to Lena. And usually when I post I get thousands of answers. I only had fourteen, but we have been talking ever since."

"Fourteen people replied?" Art asked. "What did you post?"

"I just asked if anyone knew what was going on."

Niles muttered, "I didn't even think of social media. We can see who is posting." He pulled out his phone.

"Useless," Cass said. "There is no signal."

"Really?" Niles lifted his phone. "I'm online"

Like it was a rush to a mad sale, everyone grabbed their cell phones.

"Quick," Mark said with a point to Lena. "That signal can go at any time. You have a lot of followers. Make a post. Put our police station number up. Get them to contact us."

"Got it." Lena turned her attention back to the phone. "Trixie, I can't get a hold of John and the kids. My mom is supposed to be there too. Can you try, maybe even drive over there?"

"Oh, Lena, you know I will. As soon as we get off the phone I will head right over."

"Thank you. Thank you. I'll keep trying to call," Lena said.

"Trixie," Mark said. "If you can just hang on, grab a pen, I'll get you directions to our town."

"I can do that," she replied.

"Everyone check their social media feeds," Mark instructed. "I think we need an emergency town meeting now instead of later. People need to know. We need volunteers for search teams, food supply runs, things like that."

Cass looked up to him. "You've been thinking about his."

137

"I have."

Cass smiled. "See, that's why I married you."

"Aw," Lena gushed.

Kit rolled his eyes.

"What?" Cass asked. "What is that look for?"

"Will you need us to speak at the meeting?" Niles asked.

"It would be good if you're there to answer questions," Mark said. "Right now, let's tell everyone to be at the theater in one hour. No exceptions, it's an emergency."

"How?" Kit asked. "How are we...oh. Oh." He shook his head. "So does this mean you want me to ride around making the announcement again?"

"Yes," Mark stated.

"Son of a bitch." Kit lifted the keys.

"Oh! Hey, wait." Cass stood. "I'll do it. I'll drive around and announce. I am an official police officer now."

Kit tossed her the keys. "All yours. I want to go online for the news."

It didn't matter to Mark who did it, as long as it got done. He wanted his town together, to plan together. He hoped that Trixie was one of many that would find their way to Griffin.

He found it ironic that a town that was always a communication dead zone ended up being a beacon of light in a world that went dark of life in the course of two days.

<><><><>

It wasn't as simple as just walking out the door. Trixie had to deal with the fear that had built up inside her over the course of the last few days. She didn't even realize the extent of it until she reached for the doorknob of her bedroom.

She couldn't bring herself to walk out.

She kept telling herself that she'd promised Lena she would check on her family, but in order to do that Trixie had to leave.

Yes, the doctor in Griffin told her it was safe. But that was there, what if it wasn't safe in Los Angeles?

Baby steps.

What she needed was fresh air. And if by some chance it wasn't safe, there was really nothing Trixie could do about it. Did she really want to die in the bedroom of her home? Die from starvation that would eventually come.

She walked to the sliding doors of her bedroom that led to the balcony, and with a trembling hand she slid it open.

It was warm and the breeze hit her. Trixie filled with panic when she inhaled.

Once she took that breath, she took that step.

Out on the balcony she stood there, taking in the quiet.

There were no sounds. No birds. Nothing.

She'd made it outside, sure she could now leave her bedroom.

Nothing had been packed, not yet. She'd be leaving in the morning and had all evening to gather her things.

Stepping back in, she didn't realize how badly her room smelled from lack of ventilation. It smelled like stale food and body odor all mixed with blueberry candles.

She walked across her bedroom and opened the door.

Directly at her feet was the rolled-up towel Anita had placed there.

That towel could have been the difference between life and death for Trixie. And while Anita had not answered her calls, Trixie was going to find her.

She had to.

In fact, after she sought out Lena's family, Trixie was going to locate any and all of the friends she'd made in the city.

Discover their fate.

If they had succumbed, Trixie prepared herself for the challenge. It wasn't going to be easy.

Her home was big, too big for just one person, but Trixie never had to worry about where she left her stuff and her purse was still right where she'd dropped it a couple nights before.

On the floor of the foyer near the front door.

She lifted it, pulled out her keys and unlocked the front door.

Her car was still there, badly parked out front.

She wasn't exactly sure what to expect, what was out there in the city, but the only way to find out was to go.

She got into her car, started the engine, and turned on the radio.

Nothing.

Not even static.

It was as if it had been broken. After placing the car in gear, Trixie pulled down her driveway and turned left.

Lena didn't live far.

Two or three miles.

It wouldn't be long before she would find out for her friend the fate of her family.

Trixie prayed it would be good news.

It took until the end of her street when she realized, those prayers probably wouldn't be answered.

She dashed the thoughts of breaking bad news to Lena from her mind. She couldn't think that way, but what she saw told her otherwise.

Trixie had always loved the intersection at the end of her street. It reminded her of her hometown in Ohio, a business block with shops and restaurants. Only the ones in Los Angeles weren't as simple and quaint.

They were eloquent and artsy but still, it was as if she'd driven into a small town nestled in a huge metropolis.

But things were different that day. There were no cars waiting on the light at the end of her road. No one trying to cross and blocking traffic. As soon as she turned onto the main drag, she realized it.

Every day a man stood on the corner with a sign that read 'free eye exams' promoting the expensive eyewear store, luring people in.

He wasn't there and his sign was on the sidewalk.

Cars were stopped in the middle of the road, abandoned with the doors open. A sure sign that people stopped immediately what they were doing and ran for cover, as if some bomb was going off.

In an essence it had.

She had no choice but to stop her car and pull over in front of Grinders Coffee Shop. She wouldn't be able to get down the road, everything was blocked.

It wasn't that far, she could walk. In fact, a friend of hers, Steven, lived six blocks away. He had several cars, so she'd stop and see him to borrow a vehicle.

No sooner had she exited her car, everything hit her. At first the quiet, the unbelievable silence. Not a bird, dog, or mechanical sound. Then came the horrid smell. It was rotten and sour and carried in the air around her. Immediately she started gagging and brought her shirt up to her nose. Her eyes lifted to the coffee shop, and she came up with the brilliant idea to use coffee as a smell filter while she walked.

Trixie wasn't thinking when she opened the coffee shop door; the smell was worse in there and bodies draped over tables and chairs. Latte cups were tipped over and spilled. Had they just dropped that fast?

They must have sought solace in the coffee shop, to wait it out and Trixie couldn't spend another second in there.

With a whimper of fear and pity for those people, mouth and nose covered, she bolted out.

Her legs moved fast as she raced down the street. She wanted to get out of the section of town that she loved so much.

If ever she was truly scared in her life, it was that moment. In the dead silence, racing down the sidewalk of a once bustling community that was now stripped of life.

She kept looking back, over her shoulder, as if death were chasing her, never realizing she wasn't running in a straight line until she ran smack into a parked car.

A sharp pain radiated up her side, taking her breath away as she stumbled back.

She nearly fell to the pavement, but in some figure skating style move, she spun, and jumped a little catching herself before she was injured any further.

She told herself right there to get it together. It was only the beginning of her journey, she had friends to check on, people she loved.

"I'm stronger than this," Trixie said out loud. "I'm stronger than this. I'm...." She froze when she looked at the car she had run into.

The doors were shut, the windows up tight. A man and woman were in the front seat and two children in the back.

It looked as if when the warning came, they pulled over and sealed the car instead of getting out. They all looked the same, heads tilted back, eyes bulging and wide, their cheeks sunk in. Had they passed away from whatever was in the air or simply died from heat exhaustion in the sealed car? She didn't know and didn't want to find out.

Trixie had been locked away for days, away from the horror. Now she was cast right into it.

It took everything she had not to vomit, not to crumble on the sidewalk with defeated tears.

Inhaling a deep breath of courage, eyes focused forward, Trixie walked quickly ahead, not looking back again.

As horrible as it was, that crash course in realty was what she needed. It was preparation for what Trixie faced ahead.

16.
HANGING BY A MOMENT

The sight of Eb smoking again took Cass by surprise. It was a habit he picked up as a kid and one he'd given up years before.

He stood outside the theater as people walked in, nodding his head in that 'up' way of saying hello as people passed him.

"Hey, Eb." Cass approached him. "When did you start smoking again?"

"When Ada gave me one yesterday." He looked down at it.

"She shouldn't be smoking either."

"I don't think Ada cares," Eb said. "And with all that's going on, really who cares?"

"We could be the last ones left and you have that attitude." Cass shook her head.

"So I take it no one is replying to the post?"

"That's why I'm here, I wanted to give Mark an update before he started. I've got to get back to the station, I'm on social media monitoring duty while we still have a connection."

"Who is there now?" Eb asked. "I saw Kit go into the meeting."

"Oh, Floyd."

"I thought he was watching for deer on Miller Run."

"He is. Or was. Will be again. Bill, Art's dad is up there now. He's from Texas so you know he knows how to use a gun."

Eb laughed.

"Anyhow, I'm gonna go inside, talk to Mark and get back to the station before Officer Floyd screws something up. Plus, he's got to get some sleep. He's pulling the night shift on the road. I suggested Ada, but Kit said he didn't want her up there at night. But Ada said not tonight, anyhow."

"That's because she has the two new science guys coming over to discuss the fungus."

Cass flinched a little at the oddity of that. "That doesn't even sound remotely fun."

"It'll be informative. I'm looking forward to it. I don't have anything to contribute, but hey, it doesn't hurt to know what you're up against."

"I thought…I thought it was done," Cass said.

Eb shrugged. "I thought so too, but Niles called the meeting with Ada."

"You've been spending a lot of time up there."

"Well, don't say anything, but I kinda think it's cool hanging out with the celebrity lady."

"She's married."

"I can still think it's cool. Why don't you come up."

"Maybe, if I can get someone social media savvy to cover the station." Cass looked at her watch. "I better get in there." She opened the door. "Maybe I'll see you tonight."

She walked inside where a familiar buzz rang in the air. People's conversation all meshing as one. The room was full with everyone from town. Although Cass didn't do a roll call.

She spotted Mark off to the right of the stage, Niles and Art behind him. Mark was reviewing notes in his hand. He was focused and glanced up when Cass touched his arm to alert him of her presence.

"Hey," Mark said. "Just in time."

"You have a full house and it's not even five yet."

"How about that."

"You think maybe you should have had it later? You know you're gonna deliver this news and send them home to spoil their supper."

"I had to, Cass, especially with the internet working they probably know more than me. Speaking of which…any takers on that post by Lena?"

"Actually, yeah, we got twenty-two calls so far. Six are from overseas."

"Are they coming to Griffin?"

"Hopefully. I'm gonna call them back. I want to keep looking. Keep trying some of the people that talked with Trixie."

"Good idea," Mark said. "At least I have news of survivors beyond us."

"And you know there has got to be more. There has to be."

"I agree," Mark told her. "And I better go."

"Me, too. I have to get back to the station."

"I'll get some volunteers to help on the social media angle," Mark said. "And I'll let you know about the teams. My goal today is to inform them, give them time to think about solutions, and then have another meeting."

"I hate meetings."

"I know you do." Mark tapped then pinched her on the cheek. "But you're cute about it." He turned and walked on to the stage.

"Ow," Cass joked then shook her head watching him.

"Good afternoon," Mark said. "If I can get everyone to take their seats. Please."

The mumbles quieted down rather quickly.

"Again, thank you for being here. I know this is short notice. I am very glad you came. The last twenty-four hours have been a doozy and this town has been calm and level-headed about things. Many of you didn't ask questions, that's why we're here today. To inform you, talk to you, plan with you and answer questions. Although." Mark paused to nervously chuckle. "You probably all are informed now being that the internet is back."

Immediately, the room erupted vocally, with everyone reacting rather shocked and saying, "The internet is back?" It seemed everyone grabbed their phone.

Cass again shook her head in amused disbelief. *Fucking people of Griffin*, she thought then began to head out.

That was when she heard it, everyone must have discovered the same news at the same time. She imagined they popped open their internet browsers and, chances were, their home screen and news informed them of what they had been sheltered from.

The world outside of Griffin was falling apart.

The tension swelled in the air, it was thick at first, then it grew loud.

Voices meshed together, shouting concern, a few sobs in the air.

"Did you know?" one man asked. "Were you hiding it from us?"

"Why would I hide it?" Mark replied.

"Then you knew?"

"I haven't known for long, I just..."

"You kept something like this from us!" another shouted.

"No, listen, people..." Mark tried to calm them.

"My sister lives in Tulsa," a woman cried out. "Do we know about Tulsa?"

"We don't know," Mark replied.

"I have to go." She stood. "She's all I have. I have to go find her."

"Now everyone sit!" The usually mild-mannered Mark raised his voice, loud and firm. "No one is going anywhere!"

But Cass was. That was her cue to leave and she decided to make her escape. Kit or Mark could fill her in later.

She walked down the far aisle to the front door exit, listening to Mark as he returned to a calm state and began his explanation of the situation.

She reached for the right side of the double glass doors. As she casually pushed it open, she felt an abrupt brush against her, shoving her slightly forward as someone ran out past her.

It took a second for Cass to register what happened, and just as she thought maybe someone got sick, she saw Lena in the street.

She moved frigidly, left to right, then in circles. She brought her arms tight to her body, slightly hunched over, then dropped to her knees and cried out.

One long cry.

It went through Cass because there was a familiarity in that cry, one Cass had made before.

Slowly she walked to Lena. "Lena," she called softly.

"They're *gone*," Lena sobbed. "They're gone, Cass. My mom, John, my b—" She cried out the words, "My babies. They're gone. They're gone."

The 'oh' seeped achingly from her chest as she crouched down, reaching out a hand to Lena. "Oh, I am…I am so sorry. Lena, I am so sorry."

Lena's shoulders bounced as she sobbed, grabbing onto Cass' hand that gripped her arm.

Cass was at a loss. She wanted to grab Lena, embrace her, and hold her. As she moved to do so, Lena jumped up.

"Lena."

"I can't."

Cass reached out to her but Lena swiped away her hand. "Lena."

Softly screaming out her pain, Lena spun and took off.

Cass called out once to get her to stop, but Lena didn't. She thought about chasing her, trying to get her to stop. But what would she say, truly what *could* she say?

Having been there, Cass knew no words spoken, no touch or embrace would make a difference. Not in the immediate aftermath of crushing news.

Cass let her go and let her run. She knew, before long, Lena would learn she could run, but there was nowhere far enough she could run to lose the pain.

<><><><>

She came under the guise of a fascination over the fungus, but Eb knew Lena was the real reason Cass was standing in Ada's kitchen.

Not that Lena was in the kitchen, she wasn't. Nonetheless, Cass came for her. Lena's loss and heartache hit home to Cass, to Eb as well. She wanted to be there to lend her support.

Eb knew that without her saying a word. Even if she pretended to care about the talk.

Niles was a few minutes late. Before he showed the conversation had hovered around the happenings in Griffin.

Cass sipped a cup of coffee, leaning back against the kitchen sink, watching and listening as Ada, Art, and Niles stood around the kitchen table.

"The thing is," Ada said, "you need to know why this thing is entering the blood stream. Fungus has always been the devil to work with."

Niles nodded. "I agree. This one is tricky."

"And different," Art added. "It lives a little longer."

"And highly contagious," Ada said. "While active. Tell me, Art, you said you saw results with my MMB tincture…"

"MMB?" Niles asked.

"Mad Man Bonanza," Ada explained.

"Yes," Art replied. "I did. On Mariah. She was the one I used it on first. I tried the other tinctures on other patients, but by the time I saw results on Mariah, it was too late to use it on the others." He looked at Niles. "It worked on the rash, but by then it had already entered the blood stream."

Ada released a short sarcastic chuckle. "And you said nature couldn't beat it; you needed science to beat it. Maybe if we would have done full strength. I mean, I thought for sure that was the one."

"It showed promise," Art said. "Active spores died instantly. Stopping it in its track."

"It's good stuff. It cleared up a case of jungle rot like I've never seen," Ada said.

"Still needed a science touch."

Niles looked at him curiously. "Why do you say that? I mean, I would think battling it with nature would make perfect sense since the fungus is not man made."

Eb asked. "It's not? I thought you told Cass you created it."

"In a way I did," Art replied. "I manipulated an already present fungus."

"Which one?" Ada asked.

"You wouldn't know it."

"Try me."

"You wouldn't know it and I'm not being arrogant."

"So really, what you're saying is," Ada argued, "that schooling and stuff trumps someone that really knows nature."

"I'm saying my education at Harvard and experience," Art said, "may give me privilege to more information."

"Fine," Ada huffed. "I still think going basic is the way."

"Why that one?" Eb asked. "I'm curious. Did you seek it out or did it fall in your lap accidentally?"

"I had read about it," Art replied. "And I chose it because I knew how virulent it was."

Ada laughed in sarcasm. "And you still felt you had to manipulate it?"

"If it was so strong," Eb said, "didn't it cross your mind it could be harmful to people and animals?"

"No. And there was nothing that indicated it would," Art said. "We tested it on various lab animals."

"Nothing," Niles said. "No reaction. But—"

"You didn't test the manipulated one," Ada said.

"We did," Niles answered. "We just didn't have enough time. They needed to push the extermination. They had to. By July the world stood a good chance of not only starving but losing oxygen when the pred bugs multiplied and devoured the trees."

"So we were doomed either way," Eb said.

Art nodded. "It may have happened faster this way, but the end result is the same."

"We also have to remember," Ada said, "they could have run all the tests they wanted. Sometime, fungi are funny. They mutate, they adapt. The fungus may have shed the manipulation you did to adapt to its preexisting pre-mutated state. But when the fungus was mixed in the batch for extermination, it was delivered before it could change back. An Ada theory, not sure if that makes sense."

Art bobbed his head side by side. "It does. Sort of. But you're right, they are unpredictable that way."

Cass had kept quiet, but finally she spoke, "Can I ask you guys a question?" She set down her cup. "If the spore things, the part of it that makes it spread and die within a day. If here we are with no more cases, if the threat is over, why are you even discussing how to beat it?"

"Well," Art said. "You never know. What happens—"

A loud thump rang out from the ceiling and everyone looked up.

After the pause caused by the loud noise, everyone gave their attention back to Art. Everyone except Cass.

"If something similar happens…" Art continued.

"Will you excuse me?" Cass said softly and walked out of the kitchen seemingly entranced.

No one gave it a second thought. Especially Eb—he was used to Cass just suddenly leaving a room when the most minuscule thing set her off.

While everyone else seemed to just dismiss the sound as something that had fallen, Cass felt differently.

She didn't quite know why, but something didn't sit right with her the instant she heard it. Once out of everyone's view, she picked up the pace to investigate.

It could have been nothing, but something inside of Cass screamed it wasn't. Whatever it was, it caused her stomach to twist and a wave of unfounded nervousness and fear swept over her as she made her way up the stairs.

The doors of the rooms that lined the upstairs hallway were open. All but one.

Position wise, that was the room above the kitchen. Or so Cass thought.

"Lena," Cass called out, knocking on the door. "Lena."

There was no answer and Cass, slightly out of breath, her heart beating out of control, turned the unlocked knob and pushed the door open.

As soon as she stepped inside the room, she knew her instincts were correct.

A fallen chair was the reason for the noise, the 'thump' against the floor.

It had fallen when Lena's feet kicked it over in her attempt to hang herself from the beam on the ceiling of the rustic bedroom.

One end of the bathrobe belt looped around her neck, the other over the beam. Her legs did mini kicks as her body twisted and turned left to right.

Every ounce of nervousness, fear, that Cass felt was gone the moment she saw.

"Lena!" Cass raced to her, shouting out, "Someone!" as she lunged for Lena's legs. "Someone help!"

Cass clutched both her legs as best as she could and, using every bit of strength she could muster, tried with diligence to hoist Lena's body up to relieve the pressure on her neck.

Lena fought. Whether it was on purpose or just her body's reaction to what was happening, she fought against Cass but not for long. Cass held on. Her fingers digging into the thighs of Lena's now limp body. Her shoulders and neck bearing the brunt of the weight, pushing her upward as she cried out again loud and desperately, "Someone!"

17.
IN PLAIN SIGHT

May 8

Ada stayed in the hall. She snatched a peek into the room when Dr. Craig walked out. Lena was asleep in the bed while Niles tended to her intravenously.

Her mind kept going back to the night before.

They were in the kitchen, listening to Art and his 'high and mighty' explanations. Cass has just walked out. Ada dismissed her leaving as part of Cass' personality. Whenever anything remotely reminded her of the tragedy of eight years earlier, Cass just walked out.

Ada was used to it.

She didn't think twice about the loud noise.

Even when she heard the desperation in Cass' call, still Ada didn't think it was Lena attempting suicide. In her years, Ada had seen a lot of people deal with loss. Cass was one of them. Ada knew people. She kept saying that Cass was on a one-way trip to taking her own life, either on purpose or by accident. But Lena didn't strike Ada as that person.

Eb rushed out. In fact they all did.

But Eb was fast, probably recognizing something in Cass' voice.

Cass was still hollering for help when Ada arrived at the stairs. When she walked into the room, Ada gasped in shock.

Cass fought diligently to hold up Lena's limp body. Eb reached to cut down the belt, doing so without causing any more harm. But it was only when Niles and Art entered and lifted Lena higher, that Eb was able to do so.

Once they placed Lena on the floor, Ada watched Cass feel for a pulse, then without hesitation deliver breaths.

Cass beckoned her, pleaded.

It didn't take long. Lena choked weakly with a whimper and that was when Ada summoned Dr. Craig.

Dr. Craig.

He made eye contact with Ada, now back in the present, as he pulled the door closed.

"How is she?" Ada asked.

"She made it through the night. That's a good thing."

"I knew she would."

"Right now, she's still under sedation and will be for a few more hours. She needs rest and to not move. I don't think anything is broken. We'll know when she wakes if there is a problem with the larynx. Doesn't feel it though. The ligation isn't too deep."

"What about a pulmonary edema?"

"We have to watch for a delayed one, clots, and other repercussions. She should be in a hospital, but we know that's not possible. We just have to keep monitoring her closely," Craig said.

"I did that all last night?"

"Maybe you should get some rest. Niles is a physician. He can handle it for a while. I also appreciate you getting the monitor from the veterinarian. I didn't have one."

"There's nothing really we can't do for her here," Ada said.

"I agree. I'll tell you, your fast reaction saved her life. And more so from any permanent damage. She could have suffered hypoxia, lack of oxygen to the brain. I mean, it really could have been worse. Do you know how long she was hanging?"

"It wasn't long," Ada said. "We heard the thump. I didn't think anything about it, no one did but Cass, so no more than a minute or two. She had a feeling."

"Where is she now?"

"Cass? She left. She said for me to call her and keep her updated. She's not one to hang around bad situations. But you know her."

"No, actually, I don't. I know her to see her. When she drives Mr. Algerman in for his tests. That's it. She seems to be the only person in town that doesn't come to me for treatment."

"I didn't know that."

"What about Lena's friend?" he asked.

"Yes, I uh…I spoke to her. She'll be here this afternoon."

"Good. That woman is alone and needs all the support she can get."

"Well, Doctor, she's part of Griffin now. She's family," Ada said, looking at the closed door. "And like any family member, we will do what we can to keep her going."

<><><><>

Cass did that 'speak softly to yourself' thing as she sat behind the computer in the police station. "Stir…crazy." She typed and hit enter. She cast her eyes over the screen and shook her head. Grabbing a pencil, she scratched out the word, one of many on a list.

The police station bell dinged and she looked up to see Eb walk in.

"Morning, Officer McDaniels," he said.

"Hey, Eb."

"Have you been here all night?" Eb asked.

"Pretty much. I just don't want to miss a second of connectivity while we have it."

"I get that. We just had an arrival." Eb walked toward Cass. "A young man from Texas."

"Another Texan." Cass shook her head. "What did he do drive a hundred miles an hour?"

"Man, you are a state boundary bigot. I think he said he was in New Mexico."

"Did Lena's friend show up?" Cass asked.

"Not yet."

Cass sat back in the chair and tossed the pencil. "Do we know where we are putting people in this town? Did Mark say at the meeting? I mean, after everything calmed down."

"He did. Mark handled it with his usual style. People calmed and then got kind of excited that we were spared. I mean those who were worried about family out there. He took volunteers for committees." Eb grabbed a chair and pulled it toward her. "A committee for housing, searching, food."

"Oh, good Lord. Mark and his committees. I'm surprised he didn't have a committee to have the festival."

Eb only looked at her.

"We're still having the festival?"

"Somebody asked," Eb said.

"The world is ending and they still want their festival."

"It's important. It signifies life. We're alive, Cass, when almost everyone else is dead. Speaking of which—"

Cass held up her hand. "Okay, if you're gonna talk about Lena, that is a terrible segue."

Eb winced. "It was, wasn't it?"

"Yeah."

"Anyhow, what you did. How you had that instinct. It was great."

Cass slightly pursed her lips and half shrugged.

"What? Why are you blowing it off? You saved her life."

"And she is going to be pissed. She's going to hate me, at least for a while." Cass lifted her eyes. "Trust me, I know. And I can't blame her. It wasn't like I pulled her out of the way of a moving car. I took her choice away."

"You and I both know she wasn't thinking clearly."

Cass nodded.

"So, what are you doing?"

"As I said we still have internet and I am on social media just looking for people. I thought I'd try key words." She pushed the paper forward. "Just throwing things out. You know."

"It's a good idea. Quite a list. Why don't you take a break? I'll do this for a while. You need a break and need to sleep."

"Maybe. Did you...did you volunteer for any committees?" She pulled the list back and began to type.

"Just the 'don't bury the festival' committee."

Cass laughed and hit enter. "Shit. Typo."

"No, I joined the committee to look for survivors."

"That sounds like a good one." She looked at the screen and readied to retype the correct keyword. "Maybe I'll...Whoa...Eb." She turned the monitor some. "Look at this."

It was the second time that Kit was doing dishes and it wasn't even noon. The first time was after breakfast, the second time was when an out of the blue idea to bake cookies hit him.

"I know you hear me." Kit aimed his voice toward the window where Kat sat on the porch not far from him. "Kat, I know you hear me."

Or did he?

Kat had done nothing but play on his phone since a signal came through. There wasn't anything he could look up or do. But he kept swiping through. What was he even looking at or reading?

Kit placed the final dish in the rack, shut off the tap, grabbed the towel and dried his hands. He turned and opened the fridge, reaching in for a soft drink. "You wanna soda?"

"No," a woman's voice replied. "I'll take a beer if you have one. I haven't been to bed so technically it's a night cap."

"Cass?" Kit asked shocked, then grabbed a beer from the fridge for her.

He was shocked to see her sitting on the steps of his front porch. "When did you get here?"

"Only a minute or so ago."

"Why didn't you tell me she was here?"

Kat shrugged.

"What are you doing so intently on that phone?" Kit asked his son.

"Seeing if anyone is posting anything. Survivors, you know," Kat replied.

"I'll accept that." Kit sat down on the step next to Cass. "How are you doing?"

"I'm fine."

"I heard what you did last night. Man, give you a badge and you jump right on that protect and serve."

"It wasn't a big deal."

Kit nudged her. "She's gonna give you hell."

"I know."

"How is she?"

"From what I heard, she's good. I'll stop in and see her after I get a little sleep. Get the fury over with."

"What brings you here?" Kit asked.

"Well, as you know, I've been going on social media looking for people that got the warning in time. But it's hard. Because they really only show up on your newsfeed if you follow them or are friends, so I decided to start searching keywords."

"That's a good idea." Kit nodded and took a drink. "You found something."

"I did. I was talking to Eb, typing in the word 'plant' but had a typo and ended up typing 'plane.' Apparently, two days ago, when it all went down, there was a plane. Here, I looked it up on my phone and did a screen shot of the posts." She handed the phone to Kit.

Kit read the post. "Guess vacation is over. Got word we can't land. Air isn't safe." He looked at Cass. "Wow."

"Yeah. Swipe to the next picture. That's the next post."

Kit did. "Landing in Arizona. He doesn't say where."

"He doesn't." Cass took her phone. "But someone else does. I started searching the terms airline and other words. About two dozen people were posting from that plane. They landed on a highway. They said eighty-nine. Near or past Willow Springs."

"That's only two hours north of here," Kit said. "So they're just sitting on the plane."

"Last post I could find is they weren't leaving until they were told they could. But that was three days ago and nothing has been posted since."

"Maybe their phones died or they lost connection," Kit said.

"Or they left," suggested Cass.

"Or," Kat spoke up, "they all died and suffocated on that plane."

Both Kit and Cass looked back at him.

"What?" Kat said. "If the pilot doesn't power down, conserve power to circulate air once in a while, they would have died of carbon monoxide poisoning if they stayed sealed in there. Plane's not gonna have power forever. They were probably too scared to leave."

Cass lifted her phone some. "From what I read. Yeah. It looked it."

"You're telling me because you think we should do this?"

Cass nodded. "Since Eb said you are also on the committee for search and rescue, I do. I want to go though, Kit. I want to do something besides go stir crazy in this town."

"Cass, you never leave anyhow."

"There's a difference between having a choice to leave and being stuck."

"She brings up a point," Kat said.

"Thank you for your input," Kit said sarcastically. "So just take a ride up there?"

"We don't know what's up that way," Cass said. "We should grab one of our scientists in case we see anything. Preferably the one that's a real doctor in case someone needs help."

"That's a good point."

"I mean, they may have left the plane. There are a lot of villages unregistered up that way—they could be untouched like us and those plane people could be fine."

"Maybe at one of the rest stops," Kit added. "Or…" He looked back at Kat. "Like my son said. They could be dead."

"We won't know unless we go."

"Shit," Kat cursed. "I mean shoot." He stood up. "Looks like our search online is over." He put his phone on the table. "Signal's down again."

"Let's plan this," Kit said to Cass.

Cass couldn't agree more. That was the whole reason she went to see Kit. It was something she wanted to do and couldn't explain why. It was a glimmer of hope. Now it would be one of the few chances they had to find survivors.

Their connection to the world, their short-lived blessing was gone, pretty much like everything else outside of Griffin.

18.
THESE EYES

Lena didn't really want the tea, but her mouth was dry and she needed something in her system. Niles was in the room when she woke and after asking her how she felt, he proceeded to tell her about her condition.

Lena didn't care.

She barely had the strength to get up and use the bathroom. Ada came and helped her with that, brought her a cup of tea, and helped her back into bed.

Her throat hurt when she swallowed.

It was stupid to try to hang herself. There had to be better ways. One more permanent.

She lifted her phone, looking at the pictures of her children and family. That was all she had, when the phone was gone, so would be the pictures.

"Now, I'll stay," Ada told her. "But I know you aren't wanting company."

Lena shook her head.

"Your friend will be here soon. Very soon. I hope you'll have her and…Cass is on her way here."

Lena looked up.

"She said you probably don't want to see her."

"Why wouldn't I want to see her?" It was hard to talk, her voice was raspy.

Ada opened her mouth but refrained from saying that Cass was the one that saved her, just in case Lena didn't know. But there was something Lena wasn't aware of, and Ada felt she should know. "No reason. But just so you know, Cass may be someone you want to talk to."

"Because of her children and parents?" Lena asked

"I wasn't aware that you knew."

"Eb told me before…before I found out about…" She didn't finish her sentence; she just lowered her head and wiped her eyes.

"They're good people, Lena. Both handled the situation differently. If you need to talk, they're the ones to talk to."

"Okay."

"I'll leave you be and send up Cass when she arrives."

Lena pursed her lips. It was hard to do anything but frown. Once Ada left the room, she tried to get into a comfortable position, but everything hurt and she was still a little woozy from the sedative.

She stared at the pictures, back and forth with a swipe of her finger. Each one hurting her a little more. She knew she had videos and saved voicemails but she wasn't ready for those yet.

A single knock came at the door and weakly Lena called out, "Come in."

It opened slightly and Cass peeked inside.

The moment she saw Cass, Lena remembered and knew what Ada said. Instantly, the grief turned to such a vile anger, Lena didn't recognize it within herself.

"I'll leave you alone if you want," Cass said.

"Cass, I'm a nice person, but right now I really don't want to see you." Lena kept her gaze down.

"I get it. I do. I've been there." Cass stepped inside, staying by the door. "Just know I'm sorry, okay? I'm sorry about what happened to your family. I'm sorry I took away your choice last night."

"It was my choice."

"I know. Like I said, I was there. I was angry when someone stopped me. I don't think people who want to live have any idea what it is like to want to die."

Slowly Lena looked up.

"But just because you want to die, doesn't mean you should. It took me a long time to realize that Kit saved my life and didn't just stop me from dying."

"Kit? The cop?"

"Yeah, I was bad. I didn't make any attempts on my life because I was certain I was going to die anyhow. Hell, I should have I was impaled by a piece of that truck. Right in my chest. Then I didn't. I spiraled out of control fast. Lost everything else and everyone else I held dear because I was selfish in my own pain and grief."

"There is no way I'll ever get through this," Lena sobbed.

"You'll never forget it. I won't lie. You'll learn to live with it. Learn to live with the days it all comes back. You want to hear nothing right now and I will not even attempt to tell you anything that will remotely try to make you feel better."

"Nothing will."

"No, it won't," Cass said. "Again, I'm sorry for taking away your choice. But, Lena, I'm not sorry you're alive."

Lena turned her head slightly.

"It's gonna sound stupid and cliché to say, but right now, you aren't thinking clearly. You aren't."

"Will I ever think clearly?"

"Yes, you will," Cass said. "If you don't hide behind a bad pain pill addiction." She sighed out heavily.

"It's not the same, Cass. I know you lost your family. I know you did. But it isn't the same. I didn't get to say goodbye, I didn't get to see them one last time, I won't even get to see them buried."

"I didn't get any of that either. So I know. Okay. I put my kids in the car with my parents and told them to be good. That I'd see them at the rest stop. I was in intensive care, and a nurse went to the funeral for me. I laid in bed watching it through a live video stream."

"I'm sorry."

"No, don't. I'm sorry. It's not about my grief or me, it's about you. Okay. And why can't you say goodbye?"

"Cass, I'm here. They're in California," Lena said sadly, her hands still holding the phone.

"Seven-hour drive away," Cass told her. "If you want to go. When you feel ready, well enough and up for it, then you go. Someone in this town will go with you. Eb, Ada, any number of people. They'll go and help you find your family and bury them. I'd suggest me, but it will take some healing before you can look at me and not get mad."

"Thank you."

"You're welcome. I'm here whenever. Get some rest." Cass slipped back out the door and closed it.

Even though a lot of what Cass said was comforting, Lena felt an anger toward her. She wanted to lash out, scream at Cass, but it wasn't Lena to do that. One thing Lena wasn't angry about was Cass' suggestion to go home to have one final goodbye with her family. As she held onto the phone, staring down at the pictures, she held onto the hope that one day soon, she could do just that.

<>‹›‹›‹›

When Cass said it, told her the idea and suggestion, Ada could have squashed that tomato she was washing.

"What are you, nuts?" Ada asked in a low scolding voice, standing in her kitchen by the sink.

"What?" Cass asked as she sat at the table. "It's a good idea."

"No, it's a horrible one. You couldn't suggest, maybe having a service here and having a grave here. No, instead you suggest the girl drive seven hours to her home, where even if she went tomorrow, the decomposition of them would be horrible. You want her to see that?"

"I think she'll be smart enough to know the condition."

"Cass, look…"

"No, Ada, if she wants to do it, then she should do it."

Ada shook her head and returned to washing the tomato. She glanced out the window. "Son of a bitch. Goddamn Floyd."

"What?" Cass asked.

Ada left the sink running, opened the pantry right by the back door, grabbed a rifle and walked out to the back porch.

She didn't hesitate or miss the opportunity.

If there was a deer in her garden it could be contaminated with that fungus. She lined the animal in her sights and fired a single shot that dropped it.

Cass flew out onto the porch. "Who did you shoot?"

"Not who. What. A deer." Ada marched out toward it. "You know it came from Miller Run area. Floyd is supposed to be up there catching them."

"You think it was sick?" Cass asked as she followed.

"I don't know. The color looked good, but I still need to check. Run back to the house for me and grab the green gloves on the counter."

"Yes, ma'am." Cass backed up.

Ada arrived at the deer. She crouched down to the animal, its fur was orange-brown and it was healthy looking. Not wanting to take a chance, she waited for the gloves before examining it further.

<><><><>

"And we don't know where?" Mark asked.

Kit shook his head, leaning against his desk. "Just that it's on a highway."

Niles lifted his hand. "I'll be happy to go with you and Cass."

"Cass is going?" Mark asked. "Why?"

"She wants to go," said Kit. "She's probably curious."

Exhaling loudly, Art paced. "It's been there since the fifth of May. It's now the eighth. We don't know what happened with these people. This could be a wasted trip."

"Is it dangerous?" Mark asked. "I mean…can there be a danger?"

"Yes," Art replied. "We stopped it here. But it needs a host—if it has one out there it can still be active."

"It kills its host in twenty-four hours," Niles said. "And everything else."

"You can't rule it out," Art argued.

"So what do you propose?" Mark questioned.

Kit lifted his hand when the phone rang. "Hold that thought." He lifted the receiver. "Griffin Police, Officer Modine…Yes, I am. I'm meeting with the mayor and our two new scientists. What's up?" Kit nodded. "Okay, thank you." He hung up.

168

Mark looked at him with question. "Who was that?"

"Crazy Ada. She said Floyd's an asshole and hung up. Now," Kit said. "Where were we? What is your solution, Art?"

"Me and Niles both go. You said it's only two hours. We can see for ourselves if there's a threat, and we know this fungus like the back of our hands. We go. Plus, if these people need medical attention, we can help."

Kit turned to Mark. "You know, to be honest, it's not a matter of needing permission. I just want you on board since you started the search and rescue committees. We need to establish that in the world right now, people just can't up and leave any time they want."

"I'm on board," Mark agreed. "We need to do it right. Find a way to establish communication, medical, scientific. It may seem like overkill, but you never know," he said. "We just don't know what's out there."

As if the screeching of Ada's brakes weren't enough when she pulled up behind the parked police car, she made sure she slammed her truck door hard when she got out.

Floyd, shotgun in hand, turned around. "Hey, Ada."

"You stupid fat ass, no good for nothing idiot," she blasted.

"Hey, what's with the name-calling?"

Ada walked to the back end of her truck, lifted her rifle, and slung it around her shoulder. "Thought you were supposed to be picking off deer up here, stopping them from coming into town."

"I am."

"Then how did one end up on my property?"

"I missed."

169

She back handed him in the gut as she walked by him. "Remind me never to trust you to get my supper."

"Where are you going?"

"I'm looking to see if any are up here." Ada marched forward.

"Okay! Let me know."

With a slight roll of her eyes, she shook her head as she walked forward down Miller Run Road. She didn't go too far; she knew exactly where to veer off into the woods. She knew the area well, that was why, twenty feet into her off-road walk, she stopped when it looked strange.

Something was different about the wooded area.

It was May and while everything had usually started to bloom, it was especially green. Almost as if she'd taken a hit of some hallucinogenic drug, the wooded area was too green.

The dead trees that had fallen during the winter months lay on the ground, green with a thriving moss.

But they weren't what caught her eye, it was the two large green mounds. From a distance, it looked as if someone had buried a body and it had grown over. When she walked closer, she knew what it was and it was bizarre.

Immediately, Ada hurried back out to the road and she whistled once, short and fast to get Floyd's attention.

"You find something?" asked Floyd.

"Yeah," Ada shouted. "Get on the radio, get that hot cop fill-in chief up here with those two Harvard brains. I need them here now."

After seeing he understood her instructions, Ada went back into the woods.

Kit Modine could be an obnoxious asshole and Ada realized that when she heard the blip-blip of the siren when they pulled up.

There was no reason for it other than to be annoying.

She went out to the road and saw the three of them, Kit, Art, and Niles walking toward her.

"What's going on, Ada?" Kit asked. "How come you're up here?"

"If your man Floyd had any sense of hunting I wouldn't be here," Ada said. "He let a deer slip through to my property. I shot it."

Art asked. "Was it ill?"

"No, thank God, it was fine. No signs at all of the fungus. You can check if you want."

"When was this?" Kit asked.

"About three hours ago," Ada answered.

"What took you so long to come up here?" asked Kit.

"I had to field dress the thing," Ada told him. "Didn't want to waste good meat."

"So what's up? Why the urgent call?" questioned Kit.

"This way." Ada waved her hand and led them off the road into the woods. "Whole area looks off. Lively. But not sure that's the best word. Until I saw those. There are more. But those three are the closest." She pointed to the mounds. "Go take a look."

Kit led the way, with Ada staying close to Art and Niles.

"I've seen a lot in my years," Ada said. "I have never seen anything like it."

They stopped before the first mound. From a distance, that was what it looked like, a mound of greenery, until a closer look exposed a hoofed leg.

It was a carcass of a deer.

Part of the animal had decomposed, but instead of insects and maggots devouring the flesh, it was covered with a green and golden grassy and leafy substance. Almost like a new fur, it blanketed the deer, covering it nearly completely with the exception of one leg, and part of the head.

Niles bent down closer to the face of the animal. A portion of the head remained along with the nose. The strangest part of it all was the eye. It was an oxymoron. Dead but alive. From the blank, lifeless, brown eye grew some sort of foliage. A single green wiry stem with a clover-looking end grew straight from the open pupil.

Niles crouched close to the animal in his examination, then looked over his shoulder to Art. "My God, what have you done?"

19.
EVERYTHING OLD IS NEW

May 9

When Eb was going to be a first-time father, because of one small fainting episode when they broke Cass' water, he was wasn't permitted in the labor and delivery room. That was more Cass than the hospital. He remembered that day well, pacing outside the door, waiting for updates.

He had the same feeling standing outside the motel, waiting on Art and Niles.

Bill had come out of the hotel office with updates they had phoned to him, but nothing concrete.

He had been outside the room all night, catching a nap here and there on the bench located in the smoking area.

No one told him to wait, but when Eb had found out they discovered something with a deer up by Miller Run Road, he merely was asking about it.

Art told him, "Listen, I know you talked about taking Lena to California. Not really sure how feasible that can be. You may want to hold off until we know something."

Know something? Know what? Eb wondered.

What had piqued his curiosity even more was in Ada's kitchen. Niles was there, and Lena's friend Trixie as well.

"So you're going with them?" asked Eb. "To experiment on this deer."

"I found it," Ada answered.

"But what do you know about this sort of thing?"

"Nothing. But I want to see and hear firsthand." Ada looked at Trixie. "You'll watch her, right?

"Absolutely," Trixie answered.

"Doctor Craig will be by two more times. There is soup in the fridge to heat, please try to get her to eat," Ada said. "I'll let you in on what we find out."

Eb wanted to scream. What did they find on that deer? Was it sick? Was the fungus still alive and well?

"Trixie," Niles said, "what did you see on your way here? Anything peculiar?"

"Not really. I wasn't looking for anything except driving," Trixie replied. "But"—she reached for her phone—"I did see something strange when I went to my friend Anita's house to check on her. I saw the same at Lena's house. I didn't know if this was the norm. I knew from Lena doctors were here in town." She handed him the phone. "I took pictures of Anita."

"Wait," Eb said. "You took pictures of your dead friend?"

Eb could hear the hard breath seeping through Niles' nostrils as he stared at the phone. "This is new. Show this to no one. Not yet. Not until we have answers." He handed the phone back.

"I won't."

The last straw come when Eb asked Trixie if he could see and she told him no. It was then he decided to tail Niles and Ada and had been at the motel ever since.

"Anything?" Cass asked as soon as she approached Eb.

"Nothing," Eb replied. "Like nothing I have ever seen. They have been in there all night long. Cass, they said something about me maybe not taking Lena to Los Angeles."

"For her health?"

"No, I think it has something to do with what they found with that deer. And whatever it was Lena's friend saw something like it in LA."

"How do you know?" Cass asked.

"She showed Art a picture of her dead friend."

"Oh, that's so wrong. Did you see it?"

"She wouldn't show me."

"That's even more fucked up. But you know those Hollywood types. So, we don't know?"

Eb shook his head.

"Do we know what was found with that deer?" Cass asked.

"Kit didn't tell you? He was there."

"That fucker. No, he didn't." She placed her hand on her hips and shook her head. She stopped cold when she saw Kit. "Let's ask him." She led Eb, marching to Kit before he got close to them.

"Six more people," Kit said. "Are you gonna open up your house to let someone live there until we figure out things?"

"No," Cass replied.

"What?"

"No, that would mean I would have to clean. Anyhow…"

"Anything yet?" Kit asked.

"Kit."

"What?"

"What is up with that deer Ada found?" Cass asked.

175

"You didn't see it?"

Eb and Cass shook their heads.

"Oh, man." Kit pulled out his phone. "Take a look."

Cass took the phone. "What is it with people taking pictures of…oh my God!"

"Yeah."

Cass handed the phone to Eb. "What is that? It looks like the ground grew over it."

"I know, right, and that thing wasn't dead that long. Two days. In my opinion, our two science guys know what's up."

"How do you know?" Cass asked.

"Niles said to Art, 'what did you do?'"

Eb's eyes widened. "This is crazy. So the people that started the end of the world are here, alive and well." He gave the phone back to Kit.

"According to them, the world was ending any…" His speech slowed down when Art, Niles, and Ada emerged from the hotel room. "How."

Art walked over to them, leading Niles and Ada. "We need to talk."

<><><><>

Art's audience sat in the police station patiently waiting for him to begin. Mark was there along with Bill to hear his explanation.

He felt as if he should have been giving a visual, a slide show or something, but all he had were his words and the backup of Niles.

"There really is a lot of good news about this," Art said.

"And with that," Mark added, "I hear a 'but.'"

176

Art nodded. "The four deer that Ada found were killed by OG-22X. Which is the name I gave my compound to kill the pred bugs."

"OG?" Kit asked. "Original Gangster."

The corner of Art's mouth raised. "Something like that. We found traces of OG-22X in the remains of all the deer. Dead of course, inactive. What happened to those deer, what covered those deer was not the result of OG-22X."

"Is that the 'but' leading to bad news?" Eb asked.

Art shook his head. "No, it's good news. Sort of."

Everyone groaned.

Mark paced some. "Look, just get to the point okay."

"There's more to the point, and there are facts you need to know," Art said. "For one, many of you know, the fungus I created was something already here. I merely manipulated it. So OG-22X is not my creation, it is a manipulation. The original strain alone had properties that were remarkable. The spores were active longer, it carried easier and it reproduced faster. The problem with it was it wasn't deadly. Like most fungi it covered and deteriorated things that were dead or useless—anything immobile—and could attach itself to dying things. For example, it would take over and kill a tree that was dying. The positive thing was as long as something was alive, it didn't touch it."

Ada inquired, "So you manipulated it to make it deadly?"

"Yes," Art answered.

"So immobile meaning…?" Ada asked.

"Anything not alive," Art answered.

Cass lifted her hand. "So what covered that deer and…I'll assume Trixie's dead friend was what? OG-22X?"

"No," Art replied. "What covered the deer and what we assume from images covered Trixie's friend, was the original strain."

"This thing," Ada said, "was so powerful, it shunned the manipulation like a cancer and regained its original form. Meaning, I was right, Mister I-went-to-Harvard?"

Art nodded. "You were right. Fungi are resilient. They adapt, and to adapt it regained its original form."

"We're ninety-nine-point-nine percent positive," Niles said, "that any contact with the original form is not deadly to humans or animals."

"Because we're living," Kit said.

"Exactly," Niles answered. "There are decades worth of research that back that it is non-lethal. It's a destroyer—it will eat anything dead or nonviable."

"If this thing is so strong," Mark said, "why in God's name did you make it stronger?"

"We didn't," Art answered. "We weakened it and added the property to kill the pred bugs."

"So all this research with this fungus," Mark said. "This thing has been with scientists for a while—you said decades. I take it this fungus is old."

"It is," Art said.

"Where did you get it from?" Mark asked.

"It was discovered in the arctic fifty years ago," Art said. "It dates back four hundred million years."

"Jesus Christ!" Ada exclaimed. "You brought back a prehistoric fungus?"

"We had to, we needed something strong that would attack immobile, nonviable things," Art said. "The pred bug, like OG-22X, was manipulated by man. The shell of the pred bug has such minimal biological properties that the fungi attacked it like it would a rock or dying tree."

Kit lifted his hand. "So you're telling me whatever died from OG-22 whatever...will be covered with this prehistoric fungi?"

"And some."

"Excuse me?" Kit tilted his head.

Eb groaned. "Now I know why you don't want us to go to Los Angeles or say something about the timing. This thing is spreading, isn't it?"

"I'm afraid, if I'm right," Art said, "it won't just be the deer, it'll be Trixie's friend or anyone else that died. It will be anything immobile or nonviable around them."

Cass let out a slight shriek. "Eb! Kit, we learned about this in Mr. Simon's biology class. Remember? The fungus that ate the world."

"That's true," Art said. "But it's not going to eat the world. Just everything not alive."

"Which is everything but people," Cass said. "And trees of course. How long?"

Art shook his head. "It depends how fast it spreads. It can be very fast, or it can take decades."

"We're safe, though," Mark said. "Right? I mean we don't have any more cases here."

Niles shook his head. "It's spreading, it's being carried from place to place."

"How?" Mark asked.

A loud 'whap' caught everyone's attention and everyone looked at Bill.

"Sorry." Bill hunched. "A fly."

"I fucking hate flies," Cass said.

"Well," Art said, "you're gonna hate them even more. The flies were the one thing impervious to OG-22X."

Kit's shoulders dropped as he sighed out. "And with all the dead bodies and animals…"

"Millions of flies. That fly"—Art pointed—"may have just dropped that fungus there."

Ada stood up abruptly, marched across the room to the desk, whipped a small spray bottle from her belt, and pumped a few times onto the dead fly. "Not anymore. I hit it with MMB."

Art shook his head with a dismissive look. "As much as I like to appease you, I can't. Your MMB isn't going to work against a pre-historic fungus. It's out there. It's back. Soon it will cover everything and if we don't figure out something," Art said, "Griffin will not be spared."

20.
WINDOW SEAT

Griffin, AZ

With her left hip against the kitchen sink, arms folded, Trixie tried to inconspicuously peek out the kitchen window. "She's not picking anything. She's just looking around."

Lena snapped the ends of the fresh green bean and tossed it in a bowl. "I'm sure whatever she's doing she has reason for it."

"So weird. Did you see the way she gutted that deer? She kind of scares me."

"It's called field dressing. Don't make fun of Ada. She invited you into her home and is a good woman. She has her quirks but that's what makes her awesome."

"I'm not making fun, I promise."

"Anyone home?" Eb's voice carried to them.

Trixie answered, "In the kitchen."

Eb came into the kitchen clutching papers in his hand. "Hey."

Lena looked up. "Hey, Eb."

"Good to see you out of the room."

"I had to. Did Cass and Kit leave?"

"Yep." Eb nodded. "Them and the two docs. About an hour ago. Not sure the radios will work. Mayor is manning the station just in case."

Trixie walked up to Eb. "I'm Trixie. I don't believe we've met."

"Eb. Nice to meet you. Is Ada here?"

Trixie pointed. "She's out in the garden."

Eb looked out the window then went to the back door.

"He's cute," Trixie whispered. "He married?"

"He's divorced," Lena answered.

"Ada, can you come in for a moment." Eb's hollering carried into the kitchen just before he returned.

"Everything alright…Eb?" Trixie asked.

"Yeah, yeah, I got some information." Just as he sat down, Ada returned.

Immediately she went to the sink to wash her hands. "Sorry. Was checking for the mean green." She grabbed a towel and dried her hands. "I'm clear. What's going on, Eb? Everything okay with Cass?"

"Yeah. Her, Kit, and the docs headed out to find that plane."

"Did you see them off?" Ada asked. "Was Cass wearing the emergency belt I gave her?"

"I did. And she was. Thank you," Eb said. "Anyhow, I know all of us were searching the web, social media, you name it, for survivors. It's especially crucial now that the…what did you call it, mean green is looming."

"If the two bonehead Harvardites are right," Ada replied.

"You don't think they are?" Eb asked.

Ada shrugged. "They could be. Doesn't mean we're doomed. It just means if it's coming we need to kick into action to stop it."

"Can we?" Eb asked.

"Hell yes. What's coming is natural, we just need nature to beat it. That's all," Ada said.

"The reason I'm here," Eb said, "is because we need to find people before the mean green takes over."

"Stop. Wait." Lena held up her hand. "The mean green. Is that what you're calling the green stuff growing on bodies and the deer."

"It's gonna grow on everything," Eb explained. "Art and Niles told us that it's gonna cover and break down anything not alive. Kind of like speeding up the biodegradable process. So anyhow, when we had a signal, I had Kat go on social media, like Lena, and start looking. But I just told him to print it up, instead of wasting time reading all the posts and feeds. He was looking through and he found one not far away." He handed Ada the papers. "I highlighted the conversation."

Ada looked down and read, "Anyone driving to Flag..." Her eyes lifted, then she continued. "Flagstaff. No planes. Stuck in Vegas."

Trixie exhaled a loud sigh. "Oh, I was stuck in Vegas once. Not exactly stuck there, but we missed our connecting flight because two Romanian senior citizens got confused and wouldn't leave the plane. The woman started crying and sobbing. We ended up in Boise, talk about nothing to do."

Ada shot her a glance. "Talk about having nothing to do with what is going on here," she said sarcastically.

"It kind of does." Trixie shrugged.

"Anyhow"—Eb pointed at the paper—"you can see two people offered him a ride to other places, but they stopped responding."

"He posted four more times to the post 'Anyone out there,'" said Ada. "Last one said he was going to the underground."

"Yeah, I couldn't figure that out," Eb said. "The underground what?"

"You know Vegas," Ada replied. "Heck you go there all the time for those fights. Is there a train...the underground what?"

Trixie spoke up. "The Underground."

Both Eb and Ada looked at her.

"You don't know?" Trixie asked Eb. "You go to the fights at the same resort. It's underground, has a few eating places, game room, comedy club..."

Eb sung out a long 'oh' and nodded. "Okay. I know where it is. It is underground." He looked at Ada. "Food. Probably thinks it's safer there."

"What are you gonna do?" Ada asked.

"Go. We can be there by four at the latest, we can make it back by dark or stay. Which brings me to my point of coming here," he said to Ada. "Feel like going?"

Ada only hesitated for a second before smiling. "Hot damn, give me fifteen minutes to gear up."

Eb agreed. Knowing Ada it would be interesting to see what she considered 'gear' for the trip, but she was by far the best person to take.

Willow Springs, AZ

"Oh, brother," were Kit's first words when they reached the plane.

Not 'oh, shit' or even 'damn' but a G-rated, boy scout, 'oh, brother.' Upon hearing it, Cass raised an eyebrow and turned her head to him. She wanted to make fun of him for his less than enthusiastic or alarmed reaction. After all he was pretty snide to her about her Ada-made utility belt. Instead, she snickered. "Really?"

"What?" Kit asked.

"That's your reaction 'oh, brother'?"

"Yeah."

Cass could have thought of a hundred other reactions to seeing the plane. The aircraft had been perfectly landed on the deserted highway. Cass supposed the pilot had truly wanted to keep his passengers safe, telling them to stay inside.

But the plane was not how they expected.

Most of it and the road around it was covered with the fungus. Primarily green in color with spots of aqua blue and emerald green throughout. It wound up from the road like a vine, reaching the plane and spreading across it like mold. Only spots and segments of the windows could be seen.

Cass looked to Art then Niles. "Neither of you have anything to say?"

"I didn't expect this," Niles said. "This is fast."

"I'm gonna"—Art pointed backwards—"move the church van back away from this stuff. You may want to move your squad car."

"Why?" asked Kit.

"Just…just in case it grows faster than we think," Art replied.

"Good lord," Kit said. "We're parked a couple hundred feet away. How fast is this thing gonna grow? Obviously not that fast."

"You never know. I never know," Art said as he walked backwards. "At one point it covered the world. Right here is a breeding ground. We can see that."

"Where did it come from?" Cass asked.

Art stopped walking. "What?"

"Where did it come from? I mean the plane is on the middle of the highway. How did it reach the plane?"

Art turned and walked to the car.

"What did I say?" Cass asked. "I thought it was a good question."

185

Kit slightly shook his head confused. "Cass, didn't you pay attention on the ride here?"

"Yeah."

"No. We saw this stuff the entire way here. What do you think all the green was on the side of the road?"

"Grass and shrubs."

"When's the last time you drove up this far north?"

"It's been a while."

"Yes, well, this place has been shades of brown for a long time," said Kit. He looked down. "My guess an animal was out there, it died, and the flies carried it."

"Or people," Niles said. "I mean, there's a chance they got off the plane and were sick, exposed and died out here."

"No," Cass stated. "They never left that plane. Why would they close the doors again? They're on there."

"Then they have to be dead," Kit said. "Look at it. It's not running. Even if the pilot fired up the engines every so often to circulate the air, it's not running now. It's ninety degrees."

"What if he was able to conserve," Cass said. "And we just so happen to be in that moment where he has it off."

"Cass."

"What if they found a way to let air in? I mean, if they waited the twenty-four hours, they'd be safe," Cass said.

"We all appreciate your optimism," Niles said. "Chances are they have passed. The temperature in there is deadly. They can't open the doors."

"Sure they can," Cass said.

"No." Nile shook his head. "They cannot."

"It's just fungus."

Art was returning and responded on his way back to the plane. "Just fungus. What exactly does that statement mean?"

"Don't be mean to her," Kit warned.

"I'm not," Art replied. "I'm just asking."

"Fungus. I mean like soft," Cass replied.

"Look down," Art directed. "Feel what you're standing on. Does it feel soft?" He walked close to the plane and touched it. "The surface is soft and pliable, but underneath it's hard. It adheres to the surface like cement. It's not coming off. When this fungus was discovered, they thought it was a prehistoric tree. That is how big and firm it grew."

"So it won't just peel off?" Cass asked.

"No," Art said sharply. "Weren't you listening? It adheres. You'd have to kill the fungus and weaken it to"—he held up his fingers forming air quotes—"peel it off."

"That's such a dick move air quoting me," Cass said. "No wonder Ada doesn't like you."

"Cass," Kit scolded. "Stop. Everyone stop. We tried. It was a bust. I just wish—"

He stopped speaking. In fact Kit jumped back, as did Art and Nile, and Cass shrieked at the shock of seeing a face appear in the fourth window from the back.

They couldn't tell if it was a man or woman, only a portion of the face could be seen along with the hand that reached up and pounded on the window.

"You were saying?" Cass asked with sarcasm to Kit.

"Oh my God, someone's alive!" Kit said. "We have to get them out."

"How?" asked Art. "That plane is sealed. That door is sealed."

"Didn't you say we could kill the fungus," Cass said. "Weaken it to remove it."

"Yes, but that's not as easy as it sounds," Art told her.

"Why not? It's fungus. Old or new, it's fungus," Cass said. "Just find an antifungal and spray it on."

"Cass," Kit spoke calmly. "This isn't athlete's foot."

"Same premise." She turned sharply when Art laughed. "What? You're the know-all expert?"

"As a matter of fact, yes," Art replied.

"Yes, well, if you were so know-it-all the world wouldn't be teetering on extinction right now, would it?"

"Cass, come on," Kit said. "I'm sure the man feels bad enough. Plus, he did try to stop it."

"Thank you, Officer, for defending me," Art said. "But on this, the theory of killing it is good, but we have nothing that can do it."

"I do. Good thing Ada armed me." Cass pulled a spray bottle from her utility belt and walked near the plane. "We pull the church van up here, we brought it to rescue them right, stand on it and spray around the door enough to peel off the fungus."

Art laughed and held up his hand. "I'm sorry. You're going to use a plant sprayer filled with some homemade concoction."

"She got you results before," Cass said.

"Yes, but not on a level like this."

"Well I trust Crazy Ada." Cass inched closer to the plane.

"Cass," Kit said softly. "We're gonna have to think of another way to get those people off the plane."

"I got this. We'll see if it works on this spot, if so we'll do the door." Cass pumped the spray a few times hitting the fungus, then stood there staring.

"If we're done playing with the tinctures of Doctor Quinn Medicine Woman," Art said, "Niles and I will see if we can work something out."

Kit moved close to Cass and whispered, "I swear one more sarcastic comment from him, I'm gonna deck him."

"Please do," Cass returned the whisper

"Okay," Kit said. "Let's all take a minute to try to…"

"Kit," Cass called him. "Look."

Kit spun around. The small spot that Cass had sprayed was turning from varied shades of green to a dull brown.

"It worked," Cass said with shock. "Ada's mixture worked."

Art rushed over with Niles.

"Oh my God," Niles stated with surprise. "It weakened it."

"No." Cass pulled out a screwdriver. "It killed it." She placed the flat end of the screwdriver under the portion that had changed color and smiled. It didn't take much effort to pop off the portion from the plane. It was a small section, six inches or so, but it came off. "See, like picking an eggshell from a hard boil egg."

"I stand corrected," Art said. "Ada is a genius."

"They don't call her Crazy Ada for nothing." Cass lifted the spray bottle. "Let's work on that door. And hopefully get them out."

Kit grabbed for the bottle. "And, hopefully there's enough in this bottle to pull off the task."

It was a larger spray bottle, but was it enough to get those who remained free from the plane?

21.
MIND OVER VINE

Willow Springs, AZ

An hour and a half later, with two inches of fluid remaining in the bottle, they flipped off what they believed was the last piece of fungus over the crease of the exterior plane door. Enough, they hoped, for the door to be opened. But it had to be done from inside.

They'd followed Cass' plan to bring the van over and were standing on the roof.

Kit tried to convey to the one and only person looking out the window to open the door.

It took a while to find out if they understood or even if they had the strength to do so, but the door finally cracked enough for Kit to grip onto and open it.

It wasn't easy. The bottom of the door was two feet higher than the van.

When it opened a tremendously strong odor seeped out, pelting them. It was a mixture of something sour, body fluids and death.

A skinny man, no older than thirty and drenched in sweat, stumbled to the door. He wheezed loudly, gasping so dramatically it seemed like an act.

It wasn't. His face was pale, dark circles under his eyes, and he swayed. "Tell me I won't die for breathing this air."

"Don't be ridiculous," Cass said.

"Cass," Kit scolded.

Just as she questioned why Kit was upset, the man tumbled out and onto Cass, probably expecting her to hold him up. But he was too heavy and too wet, and not only did she not hold on for long because of the weight, Cass instinctively jumped out of the way.

The man dropped to the roof of the church van and rolled down over the windshield to the hood.

"Cass, what the hell?" Kit asked.

"You expected me to catch him? I wasn't ready!"

Niles hurried to the man. "Are there more alive?"

The man nodded.

Niles peered up to Kit. "We need to go in."

"Stay with him," Kit instructed. "Art, get water out of the van."

"Kit," Niles said. "We can't just head back. If anyone else is like him, we need to find a place to give them medical attention, at least for today and then head home tomorrow."

"We will. But right now…" Kit looked at Cass. "Ready."

Cass nodded her reply.

Kit stepped up and through the door then he turned around and extended his hand to Cass. She used it as leverage and climbed inside.

The moment Cass crossed the threshold of the plane, Kit stopped her.

They had boarded on the right side, through the doorway closest to the front. It wasn't a big plane, Kit believed it was an Embraer 175, and where they entered brought them between the small galley and storage closet, directly across from the lavatory.

A good place to keep Cass from seeing anything.

"You know, what? Stay here," he told her. "Let me look first."

"I'm fine." Cass brought the back of her hand to under her nose.

"Just...stay here, okay?"

Cass agreed and Kit braced himself for walking that plane.

He didn't know what to expect but he knew what he would see. Families traveled on planes and maybe it was a sense of protectiveness over Cass that made Kit want to be the first to explore.

He could smell it...death. The air was stale and thick, the temperature was stifling hot—the fact that the young man still lived told Kit the pilot had circulated the air.

Kit listened.

He listened for any signs that meant life. A breath, cough, rustling, groaning...anything.

The lavatory door was closed and the cockpit open. It was dark. He could see the outline of one pilot slightly slumped in his seat. He wasn't moving. In fact Kit stood there, watched and listened before moving through the fuselage.

He would definitely check again on that pilot before he left.

Slowly he walked through the small first-class section. Four rows, two seats on one side, a single seat on the other. Only a few passengers were there, the remaining seats held crew.

His foot kicked an empty water bottle as he inched down the aisle.

There were many empty bottles: water, soda, juice, and wine.

He didn't need to check for pulses, he knew by looking at those in first class that they were dead.

Their faces were pale and dry, eyes sunken in, a dried white foam formed around their mouths and on their chins. All of their torsos and bellies were unnaturally distended. A sign of 'hot car death'— the temperature reached too high, and their insides slowly baked.

There wasn't enough water to save them.

But how did the man from the back of the plane survive?

Surely the temperature in the back was the same as the front? Too hot to sustain life.

And as Kit walked into the main cabin and economy section it didn't feel any cooler. It was much of the same view. Scattered bottles, snack bags…bodies.

It was a twenty-row aircraft and it wasn't until Kit hit row fifteen that he felt it. Perhaps it was his imagination, but he swore he felt a temperature change. That was when he noticed the last three rows were empty. Where were the passengers or had the rows always been empty?

"Anything, Kit?" Cass called out.

"Nothing yet…but…" Kit peered forward to the end of the craft. He saw a leg extending out from the back to the aisle. It looked like a man's leg.

He picked up the pace, slipping near sideways down the narrow aisle. When he arrived at the leg, he noticed the curled toes on the bare foot.

That wasn't all he noticed.

Early on, after they landed, someone had opened up the rear left door, realizing the twenty-four hours were up, he guessed.

It brought in fresh air, lowering the temperate on the plane, but it hadn't lasted for long and for the same reason Kit and the others never saw that the door was open. The fungus had grown over it leaving only small pockets of openings and air. The missing passengers, six in all, were gathered by the door.

Two of them were dead, while the other four, one of them wearing a pilot uniform, huddled together. Their legs twisted around each other, slightly overlapping. They grasped at the fungus, their necks arched and mouths open, aiming for the tiny pocket openings, desperately trying to suck in every bit of cool air.

They were alive, barely, but they were alive.

"Cass!" Kit called out. "Get the others. I'm gonna need some help."

Outskirts, Las Vegas

"Vegas five miles." Ada looked down at her watch. "Good timing."

"Yep," Eb replied. "I can make this drive like I'm on auto pilot. Kind of sad, though, I won't be able to do that anymore."

"Sure you can."

"Nah, it won't be the same. Although, a demented part of me kind of is looking forward to seeing the apocalypse Vegas. I think it goes back to reading *The Stand*."

"That was downtown, not the strip," said Ada.

"True."

"Cass ever come out here with you?"

"Oh, sure. But not that much. Couldn't pull her off the slots. She used to say she could lose all her thousand dollars a week for life easily. Claimed it was her addictive personality and she could easily get addicted to things."

"Well, we learned that to be true," Ada said.

"Yes, we did. Still, if she wasn't riding out for that plane, I may have asked if she would have come with me. No offense."

"None taken," Ada replied. "What happened there, Eb? I mean we all wondered. What you and Cass went through, the town hadn't seen a tragedy hit a family like that since the fire killed the Hoffer kids."

"You can say I wanted to embrace every memory and hold on to them and Cass, well, she didn't want a part of anything that reminded her."

Ada nodded. "Still, is there more to the story? I mean, we all took it as you gave up on her."

"I kind of did. It was purely selfish. I couldn't help her or save her, and I just couldn't be there when she died," Eb said. "And it was gonna play one of two extremes. Either she'd get help or die."

"She never moved on after you."

Eb laughed. "She remarried."

"Oh, stop. You and me both know that was platonic and for insurance. Mark's a good friend. If it wasn't for that good insurance, she would never have gone away for the help she got. He saved her. If it wasn't for him she'd be dead."

"Technically, if it wasn't for Kit she'd be dead, hit by the next Walmart truck zooming down the highway at eighty miles an hour."

Ada laughed. "Ain't that the truth."

"Maybe I gave up too soon. I always ask myself that. At least we're still friends. Good friends. I'll always love her. I never loved anyone like I loved Cass. Heck, who am I kidding. I never loved anyone else."

Ada reached over and tapped his hand. "You know the world. It's bad. And there is gonna be very little room for second chances. Why don't you see if enough time has passed where you're both on the same wavelength? Besides, there's not many choices, and if you don't take another chance with that wife of yours, Hot Cop is gonna snap that right up."

"What?" Eb asked with a laugh. "Kit."

"Not talking Floyd. Kit is the only hot cop in town."

"Nah, they're friends."

"He had her over for dinner twice this week. Twice mind you and the first time…" Ada nodded. "He had her over on Hamburger Helper taco night."

Eb hit the brakes. "What the hell, Ada, Kit's a friend. He wouldn't do that. Would he?"

Ada shrugged. "In a world with a population of two hundred. Who else is he gonna snatch up?" She smiled at Eb. "I'm teasing you."

"So he didn't have her over for Hamburger Helper taco night?"

"Oh, no he did."

Eb grumbled, shook his head and that was when he finally looked up and noticed. "It's here." He felt a thick heaviness upon seeing the sporadic patches of the green fungus. "I didn't think it would be here."

"Well, Art said it hits everything dead. You don't get more dead than sand and dirt."

"To me, Vegas always symbolized life." Eb continued to drive toward town. "I guess not anymore."

Willow Springs, AZ

Six.

They evacuated six more people from the plane—four women, two men, one of which was the pilot. All had been huddled by the open back exit.

Not all of those grasping for life had lived.

Kit went back and checked for a pulse of every passenger on the plane even if he knew damn well they were dead. Two of those passengers still held on for dear life. A weakened pulse and a prognosis of death shortly after.

They took the two passengers from the plane. At least they didn't have to die there like the other one hundred and two people.

Carrying them from the plane and into the van was a group effort. Art and Niles would carry the passenger to the exit, and because Kit was the strongest of them all, he would be on the roof of the van with Cass to guide the person out, then Kit would climb off the van while Niles joined Cass on the roof to lower them to Kit.

The van was running, the air conditioner pumping and they loaded everyone, a total of seven into the church van.

It was a short but physically exhausting process for them all.

"I can't properly examine them," Niles said. "Not here. Not in the van."

"We should head to Griffin," Cass suggested. "We're talking two hours."

Nile shook his head. "That's fine. But the faster we start hydrating them, the more chance they stand of survival."

"Niles," Cass said with some disbelief. "They've been on that plane for days. Would two more hours really hurt?"

"It may not hurt a couple of people, it will others," Niles stated. "We made it here literally in the nick of time and we must do what we can to help them survive. This world has lost too many and too many couldn't be saved. These people can."

"How is it possible?" Kit asked. "I mean we don't have any IVs."

"Old-fashioned way," answered Niles. "We get them to drink, we literally drop it in their mouths." He looked at Cass. "If you want to go back to Griffin, either of you, go. Art and I can handle it."

Kit shook his head. "No, we'll stay. We'll help. We're talking what? A few hours? Overnight?"

"What about Kat?" Cass asked.

"He knows there's a chance we won't be back until tomorrow," Kit answered.

"We passed a town," Niles said. "Not a really a town. More like an abandoned highway stop with some businesses."

"That's Cameron," Kit replied. "They have a small church there. We can lay these people down in there. Find fluids at the restaurants. It's only a couple miles."

"Then that's what we'll do, Officer, thank you," Niles said.

"Good. Cass and I will head to the restaurant. You situate the patients."

"Thank you again, Officer."

Kit gave a quick tilt of his head to the left as a signal for Cass to walk with him.

"Man, they just refuse to call you Kit," Cass said.

"They will eventually."

"Kit." Cass reached out, grabbed his arm, and stopped him. "You did really good back there. You alright?"

"Yeah, I am. It was…it was tough. All those people, Cass. They just suffered because their source of information shut down before they knew that in order to live all they had to do was open that door right away." He started walking again.

"They did, Kit. They did. They just didn't leave and the fungus grew over their only open door."

"It was a horrible death for them." Kit approached the squad car and stopped dead.

"Kit?"

He walked around to the passenger's side, then away from the car a few feet. He stopped at the fungus that covered the ground. He stepped on it, stomped it a few times, then looked around again.

"Kit, what the heck are you doing?" Cass asked.

When he glanced her way there was a look of concern on his face.

"What's wrong?" Cass asked.

"Nothing. I'm probably mistaken."

"What?"

"Nothing." Kit cleared his throat. "Let's just head to Cameron." Before returning to the driver's side, he opened the door for her.

While Kit got in, Cass hesitated. She peered out to the fungus, then back to Kit as he started the car.

She wondered what he saw, and even though he said it was nothing, Cass didn't believe him. He did see something, because a typically unwavering Kit wavered, and that just didn't happen for no reason.

Las Vegas, NV

The only green Eb had seen in Vegas was the decorative planted trees and shrubbery, his money leaving his hand, and the huge Grand Hotel, which, ironically, was Eb and Ada's destination.

As it had in the desert area, the fungus had arrived.

It appeared in patches on the street, crept off the overhead walkways, and the castle-like hotel looked like something from an old *Highlander* movie.

It wasn't everywhere, not on every part of every building, but enough that it changed not only the entire look, but the feel of the city as well.

Eb pulled the pickup to the parking garage entrance, stopping just before pulling in to assess if it was safe and if he could get through.

Fungus had begun to form on the arch of the entrance.

He and Ada both stepped out, a rifle strapped over her shoulder.

"Oh, God." Ada coughed. "Is that humidity?"

"Like a jungle," Ed replied and blew softly through is lips. "I don't want to think about how bad it will be if this city gets covered."

"Anyone stop to think how this will affect the atmosphere?"

"Jesus," Eb said. "I didn't think of that. It could kill us all."

"It could. Right now…why did we stop?"

"It's growing." Eb pointed to the archway. "It's just a question of how fast it's growing. What if it's growing so fast it blocks us in?"

"I don't think it will grow that fast."

Ed reached up and touched it. "Feels like grass but"—he slammed his hand on it—"hard as rock." He tried to pull it. "Doesn't move."

With a 'hmm,' Ada walked back to the truck. Eb watched her reach in the back end and pull out a backpack type item that looked more like what the Ghostbusters would wear.

"What the hell is that?"

"Got this from Pete Jones when he quit the exterminator business. Here, hold my rifle." She handed the weapon to Eb then placed on the pack, pulling out the hose with the squeeze handle trigger.

"What is in there?"

"My antifungal mixture."

"You think it's gonna work on something of this scale?"

"Building?" Ada shook her head. "No. Never be enough of it. But for a doorway. Sure."

"It works?"

"Yep."

"You tested it?" Eb asked.

"You know that smart shit Art didn't want to admit it worked, eventually he did, but it was too late for those who got infected. When he got that deer and brought samples from it, we tried my mixture on one of the samples and damn if the green didn't turn brown. Still he wouldn't admit it."

"Maybe because he knew it wouldn't work on more than a sample."

"Doubt me. Go on." Ada aimed and squirted a portion.

Eb placed his hands on his hips. "Nothing is happening."

"Give it more than five seconds goddamn it."

Eb exhaled almost impatiently then widened his eyes when he saw the area she'd sprayed began to die off. "It's crazy."

"Yeah, isn't it. I don't think it will stop it from growing back. It might. We didn't get that far. But it's something…" She grabbed her rifle from Eb's hand and, using the butt, hit into the dying portion. It cracked and fell to the ground. "There. We can go in. We won't get stuck even if this crap grows a mile a minute." She turned to head back to the truck.

"Wait," Eb told her. "Just in case it does grow that fast. Spray again on the empty spot."

With a shrug, Ada did and for good measure, she sprayed an untouched area.

They returned to the truck and drove inside.

Where they needed to go was a level down. Eb was all too familiar with it. Inside the garage were pockets of the fungus. It grew on some of the cars. Mainly the ones closest to the doors and openings. Eb picked a spot more central and they walked across the lot to the set of double doors where a sign overhead read 'The Underground.'

"Sounds seedy," Ada said.

"It's not." Eb, with a smile, carefully opened the door. "Hopefully this guy didn't go nuts."

"Hello!" Ada called out. "Anyone here?" She looked at Eb. "What was his name on the social media post?"

201

"Fishman and some number."

"Hello! We're looking for Fishman," Ada called out again.

It was a dark hallway and surprisingly the power was still on. Eb knew someone was there because he could smell food.

After Ada called out once more, they heard clumsy bangs and thumps, followed by running footsteps.

Just as they turned the bend in the hall, a man appeared.

"Oh my God," he gushed excitedly. "Oh my God. People." He wore jeans and a tee shirt and to Eb, the guy had kept himself together while waiting.

"I'm Eb." He extended his hand. "And this is Ada."

"George. I'm George and I'm so glad to see you. I didn't think anyone was left in the world."

"Are you the only one?" asked Ada.

"Here. Yeah. In Vegas. I don't know. But I do know everyone around here either died or left. I was in my room when the news said to stay inside. I didn't think that many people were exposed to it, but everyone I spoke to got some sort of rash or sick."

Ada nodded. "It's caused by a fungus and when the spores are active they spread. That's what happened. We saw your post."

"Thank God. I just wanted to go home but when I realized I should have just taken any ride, it was too late."

"You didn't think of hitting valet parking?" Eb asked. "Find some keys. Find a car?"

"Um...no. I don't even know what's going on out there."

"It's bad," Eb replied. "I know you wanted to go to Flagstaff. We're not sure if it's okay, but we can try to take you there. We're from Griffin."

"I appreciate it. I do. Let me grab my stuff." He took off darting into one of the fast food restaurants.

Ada turned to Eb. "Should we drive around looking for people?"

"I don't know. Maybe drive slow and beep the horn to draw attention. Who knows I...can you..." Eb pointed back. "Can you wait for him? There's something I want to see."

"Sure."

"Thanks." Eb turned to his right and headed toward a staircase.

Ada watched Eb leave. She had no idea what he was doing. She waited for George who took a few minutes to gather his things.

"Where did he go?" George asked.

"Up."

"Shit."

"What?" Ada asked.

"Everyone is dead up there. I wouldn't go up there."

"George. Wait here. I'll be back."

"Didn't you hear me? It's dangerous."

Ada lifted the spray bottle to her pack. "I'm armed. I'll be right back. I promise."

It was strange, there were lights on and she could hear the struggling sound of the escalator as it battled the growing fungus that clung to the railing. Like Eb, she took the stairs.

It brought her to a set of glass doors and she entered into a wide, bright lobby.

The roped-off areas used for check-in had toppled over. Abandoned luggage was strewn across the floor with paper and other garbage. The main doors of the hotel were shattered and the glass looked like someone had dumped an ice machine.

It wasn't silent and that surprised her.

Blings and bleeps along with music carried to her. She realized once she entered the casino that most of it was flowing from an automatic sequence on each video slot machine. A sequence that showed the biggest hit one could get—a way to entice players.

And people still played as long as they could, literally.

They slumped dead at the machines, credits still on there.

The carpet beneath her feet felt strangely damp as she walked.

"Eb," she called out.

"Over here."

A little farther and she found him. He was seated at a slot machine, one with pyramids and Egyptian symbols on it. His hand touched the button and the reels spun.

"Eb, what are you doing?" Ada asked.

"So close to a bonus," he said. "I had a twenty in my pocket."

"Eb, sweetie…"

"Shit." He hit the button and shook his head. "So close. Did you see?"

"No. We have to go."

"I know," Eb replied. "I just know if I hit max bet I'll hit the jackpot."

"Eb, honey…did you honestly just come up here to gamble?"

Eb's hand slid from the machine and he turned slowly to face her. "No, I came up here to experience this one more time. Because it's done and it won't be long before it's all gone. Nothing left to see."

"We don't know that, Eb."

"Yeah, yeah, we do. Ever see the movie or read the book by Stephen King called *The Langoliers*?"

"Yes, what's that got to do with anything?" Ada asked.

"Everything. We're living it. Only instead of some mysterious thing eating up our yesterday, this fungus," Eb said, "is eating up our tomorrow."

<><><><>

Steven was his name. The first airplane survivor, the one to peek through the window and stumble out. He cried out in pain, sitting up as he did so in the fourth pew of the small church.

"It's okay," Art told him. "It's a muscle spasm. I promise they'll stop once we get you hydrated. Cass?"

Cass had been looking at those they brought in, their makeshift beds in a house of worship. That had to afford them some peace, she hoped. "Yeah, I'm sorry." Carrying a bottle of juice, she hurried over to Steven.

"See if you can get him to sip," Art said. "Thank you."

"Sure." It was no secret Cass was out of her element giving care to people. "Can you sit up some?" she asked Steven and then helped him.

"Sorry. Thank you."

"It's okay." She held the bottle near his mouth. "We just need you to drink."

"I...I conserved mine," he said, cringing as he drank. "They passed out everything to everyone and we were in charge of our own rations. It wasn't much."

"The heat had to be unbearable. It's a miracle you survived that."

"It was hot and then they opened the door and it helped. We hoped the night air would, you know, cool things. It didn't. But..." He took another sip. "By the time we woke up yesterday morning the door was covered."

"And it wasn't covered when you went to sleep?"

He shook his head. "It got worse during the day."

"Can you excuse me?" Cass asked, making sure he had the bottle of juice well in his grip. "I'll be back."

205

She backed away, heading toward the aisle.

"Cass?" Niles called out. "Where are you going?"

"There's something I need to do. I'll be back."

When she heard Steven say that door was covered overnight, it made Cass worried. The fungus was consuming everything. If Griffin managed to remain unscathed, there would be nothing left in the world to take. No resources to run to. Nothing. She went into some weird flight or fight mode, or more so like a panic shopper and she knew what she had to do.

She stepped from the church. The squad car was parked in the middle of the street, the trunk was open, but she didn't see Kit.

She crossed the road and walked into the one truck stop called The Trading Post. A little store and restaurant. It was where she'd grabbed the juice for the airplane people.

There were a lot of items in there, but Cass went into the back of the diner to the kitchen. She peered around, she didn't know exactly where it would be, but knew it was there. It had to be.

She found it next to a small back office marked, 'manager.' It was the pantry.

Inside was her jackpot. Large cans of produce, boxes of pasta and rice, cases of water, cereal. Figuring she'd start to her left, she loaded up her arms with boxes of pasta and carried them outside.

As she approached the squad car, grateful the trunk was open, she saw Kit walking toward her. He had something in his hand but she couldn't make out what it was. She basically just dropped the pasta into the trunk, then arranged them in a flat manner to add more items.

"What are you doing?" Kit asked.

Cass jumped. "Oh, sorry. Getting supplies. There's more in there."

"That's a good idea," Kit said. "Get what we can. Surplus."

"This place is untouched."

"For now."

"What do you mean?" Cass asked.

"You heard Art and you even said you remembered it from science class."

"The fungus that ate the world," Cass said.

"Let's hope history doesn't repeat. How the hell did you remember that?"

"Who knows. I remember weird shit. What are you up to?"

"Just an experiment." Kit tossed something in the trunk.

Cass heard the thunk and looked down to see a can of spray paint. "You doing murals now?"

"No. It's an experiment. I'll let you know about it as soon as I figure out if it was merited to even try."

"Well what is it?" Cass asked.

"It'd rather not. I'll help you forage supplies."

"Forage." Cass laughed. "That's an odd choice of word."

"Yeah, well, I'm pulling out all my survivor vocabulary."

Cass led the walk back to The Trading Post. "Like scavenging."

"Survivors."

"Marauders."

Kit nodded. "Good one. Speaking of survivors..." He stopped before the three-step wooden staircase of the post. "How are they?"

"Dehydrated. Too bad they aren't like fruits we can just stick them in water and plump them back up."

"That's terrible."

"I know. My bedside manner lacks. Some are in pain. Having muscle spasms, some delirious. Kit..." She stopped. "Steven, the one guy, he said the fungus grew over the door overnight. I mean that's when I started grabbing supplies. It just clicked something in me. Do you think it's possible it can grow that fast?"

"I'm not the scientist. But I think it could."

"I wish there was a way to find out. Some way, so we have something to tell the people in Griffin."

"I'm working on it," Kit said.

"The spray paint?"

Kit just stared, then turned away from the post and merely told Cass to, "Follow me."

Cass stared down at the red line painted not only on the road, but where it went off to the berm like a bookmarker.

"The fungus growth on the side of the road was a half mile out," Kit said. "Northeast. A mile and a half north."

"To our plane."

Kit nodded. "I went off the northeast one, because it was closer, and every hundred feet, I painted a line. It's raw science, but it will give us an idea how fast this is moving."

"Weather conditions can change that."

"Of course, and Art said it doesn't hit anything alive. That's why it didn't touch the trees on Miller Run."

"Oh my God, Kit, Miller Run is so close to town."

Kit nodded. "Too close. But we can't plan to do anything until we know what we're dealing with and our scientists know as much as we do. I'm just not sitting around to wait."

"Whatever Ada put in that spray bottle worked."

"It did. Sadly, I don't think there can be enough of Ada's formula to stop what is happening to this world."

"We only need to stop what is happening from happening to Griffin," Cass said.

"If that's even possible. But...we can try. We will try. I'm not giving up." Kit exhaled a heavy breath. "Are you?"

22.
HEADLIGHT

Griffin, AZ

There was no fanfare when Eb and Ada returned. He didn't expect there to be. Griffin looked normal. A mellow state on the verge of evening.

When he pulled into town, he saw Mayor Mark standing by his black, expensive SUV. Mark waved for Eb to stop.

He pulled the truck over and stepped out with Ada.

"How was Vegas?" asked Mark.

"One survivor. He's in the truck," Eb replied.

"How is he?" Mark asked.

"Fine."

"Well, let's not take a chance," Mark said. "Doctor Craig set up a little hospital at the bingo hall. Take him over to have him checked out just to be sure."

"I'll do that," said Ada. "Then I want to head home. Check on Lena."

"She's in the bingo hall," Mark said. "She wanted to do something."

"Even better," said Ada.

"Hey, Mark, Vegas…it's got that stuff," Eb said.

"The mean green, as we call it?"

Eb nodded.

"How bad?"

"Getting there. I took my shortcut, but I'm thinking we need to go to Seaver, see the state that's in. Flagstaff, too."

"We're already ahead of you on that. Bill, Art's dad, and Kat took a ride to Seaver and Walt to Flagstaff. Looks like mean green is starting there. It's crawling on the outskirts. Seaver not so much. Kat took some pictures. I think we should go back. Get what we can from there. You interested in going?"

"Absolutely," Eb replied.

"Good. I wanna put together teams. Send people out in all directions. We need to get a grip on what we're dealing with and where this thing is."

"That's a smart idea. What did Cass and Kit say about Willow Springs?"

"They aren't back yet."

"How?" Eb asked. "They're closer than we were. How are they not back?"

"They aren't."

"You aren't worried?"

"No," Mark answered. "And neither should you be. They were going after a plane of people. They said if the health of those folks wasn't up to par, they were staying put until they stabilized them. That's what the doctors said."

"It's bad out there. I don't know…"

"Eb. You made it back, right?" Mark reached out and grabbed his arm as assurance. "They will too."

Eb pacified him with a nod and headed back to his truck. He drove as far as the bingo hall, a block up the road. Getting there at the same time as Ada and George as they stepped inside.

The bingo board was on the stage, though it wasn't lit up. And across the small hall cots were set up in neat rows of five.

Eb saw Lena smoothing out the blanket on one of the cots and he walked up to her. "You helping out here? That's a good thing."

"I couldn't just sit there."

"I understand."

Lena looked beyond Eb. "Ada is with someone."

"We found him in Vegas."

"Is that stuff there?" Lena asked.

"It is and growing fast."

"Which means it's taking over everywhere."

"It is so bad…I know you're just recovering, but I also know you want that final goodbye."

"I do."

"I'm thinking your trip to LA really can't wait."

Ada walked up to the pair. "Doc Craig is looking at George. Although I don't think a thing is wrong with him." She put her hands on her hips. "I thought the plane people would be here."

"They're not back yet," Eb said with concern. "We left after them, went farther and they aren't back."

Lena interjected. "Doctor Craig said some of those people could be dehydrated, heat stroke, they may not be able to travel right away. That's what he said."

"If they stay there too long," Eb said, "they may not be able to get back. What if something is wrong? What if they need help?"

"Eb," Ada said his name calmly. "If you're thinking about going out there, don't. There's no need. If they aren't back by tomorrow then take a ride out."

"What if they need help now? Cass is all I've got."

"And she'll be here tomorrow. You were fine with her leaving. Now you're not? What changed?" Ada asked.

"I saw what was out there."

"She'll be fine," Ada reassured him then turned and walked away.

"Eb," Lena said his name softly. "If you feel you need to go, you do what you have to do. A missed chance is not one you get back. Trust me."

"Oh, I know that. I do. And we're gonna get you back to LA before it's too late, too."

"Thank you. I know I'll get there. If it's the last thing I do. I need to see my family."

"Hey, Eb." Mark's voice carried across the bingo hall.

Eb turned around.

"Bill wants to head back to Seaver. You still interested?"

"Um...yeah. Yeah." He looked at Lena. "Thanks again. I'll see you in a little bit." Eb waved to Ada and walked to Mark. He would take that ride to Seaver, trying not to worry about Cass and the others. Hopefully, they'd be back by the time he returned. If they weren't, he wasn't sure what he would do.

Cameron, AZ

It wasn't getting any cooler, at least it didn't feel it to Cass. It was more humid than she'd ever felt, and she sat outside The Trading Post hoping the night air would cool her.

213

Inside the air conditioning ran, but she just didn't want to be in there.

She had a lot on her mind.

One of the passengers had died, another was critical. She was irritated because she knew they stood a better chance in town.

But there was no getting through to Art and Niles.

The heat and the death weren't what lay heavily on Cass' mind though. It was the fact that the fungus was growing exponentially fast; the possibility of total human annihilation loomed on the horizon and Cass…she just didn't care.

Live or die, she felt it didn't matter. Maybe when the time drew nearer she'd care.

Her thoughts went from Kit's experiment to the sky. It was clear, star filled and bright.

She didn't turn around when she heard the door to The Trading Post open, or the sound of footsteps on the porch. She did, however, look up when the beer was extended to her.

The second her hand touched it, she smiled. "It's cold. Thanks."

Kit sat down next to her. "You alright?"

"Yes. Thank you." Cass sipped her beer. "Oh, that's good."

"You didn't eat."

"I did. Just not much. It's not…Hamburger Helper tacos."

"No, it isn't."

"Did the two brainiacs agree to leave first thing in the morning?"

"They did. I want to also keep stashing what we can in the squad car."

Cass nodded. "I'll help. I'm gonna finish this first."

"So, what are you doing? Just sitting here."

"Thinking."

"About?" Kit asked.

"The Space Station."

"What?" Kit asked.

"See that?" Cass pointed. "That really bright twinkling star. That is the Space Station and a week before all this started we sent up a new crew. So right now, there are ten people up there, looking down at Earth. Knowing the fates of their families and watching as this world physically changes, all while...all while, they'll never get home and they know it."

"Wow, that is deep."

"I can be deep." Cass brought her beer to her lips.

"Maybe they're up there thinking about a way to get home."

Cass laughed.

"That's funny?"

"Yes."

"That's some of the smartest people in the world up there."

"And we have some of the smartest people in the world right over there." Cass pointed to the church. "Sometimes really smart people have a hard time thinking outside the box."

"I think those two are the exception not the rule."

"Maybe."

"But I agree with you, Art and Niles are not gonna be the ones to get us out of this mess."

"If we can," Cass said. "This may be it. This may be the way we go out. Like one of those movies where everyone knows the last day is at hand. Some go nuts, some just kick back."

"I don't think there's a right or wrong way to go out."

"How are you going to do it?" Cass asked. "I mean, if this is really the end. How are you gonna spend you last day?"

"With my son."

Closed mouth Cass nodded sadly, then drank her beer.

215

"Cass, I am sorry for what happened to you and Eb. I don't think there is a single person who doesn't wish with all their hearts that they could change it."

"I know."

"I wish you and I were having days where we argued about my boy not treating your girl right, or Jordie telling you Kat won't dress right for the prom. All that instead of did the chief or didn't the chief act inappropriately in cell number three."

"You really think of this?" Cass asked.

"I always think about what could have been."

"Me too. At least now I do. For a long time I didn't. For what it's worth, I wish we were arguing about that stuff too. But…if the end does come you aren't alone."

"Neither are you."

"Nah, I'm alone. I don't have anyone special. I suppose I could grab Eb and hang with him. Sort of my default apocalypse buddy."

"That's not fair."

"Life's not fair, Kit. I blame myself. I mean, yeah, Eb left me, but I shut down. I didn't open my heart to anyone."

"I hear you on that. I did the same thing," Kit said. "It's been so long…" He peered up to the sky. "I'm not sure I am even capable of feeling anything. It's like I'm numb."

"Me too." Cass rolled the beer bottle between her hands, then set it down. "Hey, Kit."

"Yeah."

"Kiss me."

Kit nearly choked on his beer with a laugh. "What?" He faced her.

"Kiss me. Let's see if I feel anything. See if you do."

"Cass, if you're wanting to deliberately prove you're emotionally dead, us kissing is the way to do it."

"Way to make me feel wanted."

"It's not about being wanted," Kit said. "It's about chemistry. Attraction. You wanting to see if you feel anything has to be tested with someone you're more than friends with."

"Yeah, you're right. We're too good of friends."

"It would be weird."

"Oh my God, Kit, okay, I get it." She reached for her beer again.

"You know what? Fine."

"Fine?"

"Yeah, let's try. Can't promise it will be any good."

"Simple would work." Cass turned and faced him.

Kit put down his beer and rubbed his hands together. He took a breath and cleared his throat.

"Why are you clearing your throat for a kiss?"

"You're not making this easy, Cass."

"It's not supposed to be easy. It's supposed to awkward and strange because it's us. And we'll never mention it again," Cass said.

"Never mention it again?" Kit asked.

"Never."

"It's like we're kids playing spin the bottle or something."

"Kit, don't make me come in for the kiss."

"Okay." Kit tilted his head left to right as if warming up for an exercise.

"Oh my God."

Then, tilting his head to the right, he leaned into Cass and gently and ever so apprehensive, touched his lips to hers. The kiss was quick and he pulled back, but only a little.

Cass wanted to laugh. She wanted to giggle, but she couldn't. She glanced up, her eyes meeting his and again, slowly Kit leaned into her.

The second kiss started out just as slow, but he didn't pull back or stop and neither did Cass.

Within a moment, Kit took control, taking it from innocent to widening his mouth for a gentle sweeping kiss. It was nice, sweet, but it didn't last long before something happened.

Bam.

The intensity instantly erupted.

For both of them.

Kit's hand rested on her cheek, locking his fingers within her hair. He pulled her closer and Cass grabbed onto him. The kisses were deep, filled with an unexpected passion while their bodies clumsily tried to figure out what to do.

Cass pulled Kit into her, and he grasped her tight. The weight of Kit pressed her against the railing of the porch. His hand squeezed her thigh as he delivered every kiss as if he were trying to breathe her in.

Then a throat cleared, loud and long, causing them to spring apart.

After a second clearing of his throat, Art smiled. "I did *not* see that coming. Excuse me, I just need to get through you two to get a soft drink."

Kit and Cass both slid opposite ways, each grabbing their beers and sitting apart.

Art walked through them. "I'll be right back out. Just in case."

There was an awkward silence, both Kit and Cass brought their beer to their mouths.

"I don't know…" Kit showed his bottle. "How these didn't spill."

"Tell me about it. Good position and placement."

Kit chuckled as he tipped the beer into his mouth. After his drink, he slowly brought it down. "Hey, Cass. You know how we said kiss and never mention it again?"

"Yep. And I swear I meant it. I won't mention it again."

"Can we not do that. Can we not...not mention it."

Cass looked at him curiously. "What do you mean?"

"I'd like very much to not forget that happened. To be honest, I'm surprised by it, very pleasantly surprised."

Cass smiled. "Me too."

Just as they leaned back in toward each other, the door opened again.

"Told you I'd be right back out." Art stepped between them and off the porch. "You may continue."

Cass shook her head, blushing some. She brought in her bottom lip and leaned back to Kit. Only this time, he stopped. He sat upright, his eyes moving away from her.

"What is it?" Cass asked.

He stood, reaching to the porch for the rifle. "Headlights."

Cass stood and Art stopped walking and turned around.

"You don't need to aim that," Cass said. "It's Eb."

"Eb?" asked Kit.

"Eb?" repeated Art. "Wow, this just got a whole lot more interesting."

Cass stepped farther into the road as the truck slowed down and stopped.

Headlights still blaring, the driver's side opened and Eb stepped out.

"Eb?" Cass walked to him. "What the hell?"

"Eb," Kit said. "Why are you out here so late?"

"No one could get ahold of you. I was worried, Cass," Eb said. "I was worried about you."

"Eb," Kit said. "She's fine. I'm here. It's awesome that you're worried but you didn't need to come out."

"Actually…" Eb stepped back and turned when the passenger door opened. "It was one of two things. Either you guys were in trouble or you had sick people from that plane. Doctor Craig figured you'd need supplies."

Craig stepped from the passenger side, lifting his hand in a wave.

Art walked to Eb. "We were stabilizing them and bringing them back in the morning."

"We get that, but there's not gonna be time to get the patients situated, so we're jumping on it now. Craig brought IVs and stuff," Eb explained. "Tomorrow morning at dawn Mark has us all assigned to teams. We're spreading out. North, south, east, west. All directions to survey and see how close this thing is to us and from where it's coming."

"Kit was using spray paint," Cass said. "Marking lines. This stuff moves fast."

"We know. We just can't figure out how fast. A lot of factors play into the spread," Eb said. "But if we don't move tomorrow and figure out a way to stay alive, like now…it will be too late. This is our Alamo. Our last stand." Eb looked at Cass, then to Kit and Art. "We're out of time."

23.
MARK, GET SET, GO

May 10

Griffin, AZ

"Honestly, Mr. Mayor," Art said, "had Craig not come out last night and brought the IVs, we would have lost three of these people. It was a good call."

Mark looked tired, the sun had just started poking in the sky and all he'd had was a nap at the station. He peered around the makeshift hospital bingo hall watching as Niles, Cass, and Craig help the new people into the beds. "I'd like to take credit for sending him but that was Eb. He was being a little protective over his ex-wife."

"She was fine."

"No doubt. Well, let's get these people well and strong. We'll find them a place to live, get them what they need. I have the crews going out today. Twelve of them. I want them to go as far as they can. Report what they see. We'll have a big meeting tomorrow to figure it out. I need you guys working on this fungus. We can't have it reach Griffin."

"It's not deadly. It's destructive. It might come down to how we live with it."

"That's unacceptable," said Mark. "We need to learn how Griffin can live without it. Thanks, Doc." He gave a swat to Art's arm and walked over to Cass. She had just finished covering a woman with a blanket. Cass stepped back, looking as if she needed a break. She wiped the sweat from her brow and stood almost defeated, with her shoulders slumped.

"Get some sleep," Mark said as he approached her.

"What?" Cass laughed as she turned around. "I'm fine."

"You look beat. Sleep would help."

"I slept a few hours. I'm good. Just a little physically worn out." Cass smiled. "Thanks for your concern."

"I'm always concerned about you, Cass."

"That's because you're sweet. How are *you* doing?"

"Stressed. I'll be better once we get an idea of what's going on. We have…" Mark exhaled and dropped his voice to a whisper. "A damn prehistoric apocalypse is happening here. Tell me that isn't the shit."

"If we have the time, we'll beat it. We'll protect Griffin."

"Bingo. No pun intended to our location now. But time is the key word. You aren't going out, are you?"

Cass shook her head. "As much as I would like to, I'm with Ada on ration committee. Set up a stockpile place. But we'll be at the meeting tomorrow."

"Where is Ada now?"

"She's home, making up her concoction so everyone can take it out today. She'll need stuff to make more, you know. She doesn't have endless supplies."

"I'll put that on my list of things to worry about." Mark stepped back and stopped. "It really works?"

"Yeah it does. At least on the little areas."

"Crazy Ada." Mark shook his head with a smile. "Why doesn't that surprise me?"

He made his way through the bingo hospital and to the door.

When she herself turned to leave, Kit walked in the door.

"Hey." She walked up to him. "I thought you were headed out with Floyd."

"I am. We're going south."

"Prescott?"

Kit nodded. "I have a feeling we may find life."

"I'll keep my fingers crossed. What brings you by? I was just headed to Ada's."

"I wanted to see you. Is that...odd?"

"A little." Cass smiled.

Kit cringed. "Anyhow. How about when I get back we do some Hamburger Helper tacos?"

"It's not Monday."

"I'll make an exception."

"I'll be there."

"Can we take you to Ada's? Are you done here?" Kit asked.

"Um...yeah. I am. And thanks. I'll take that ride." Before walking out, Cass did a visual check. Everyone seemed to be settled. Even though she hadn't truly stopped for days, she wanted to head over to Ada's, start her work there. Everyone else was constantly busy so there was no reason Cass should be an exception.

<><><><>

It was hot. Too hot for six in the morning. Beyond the rows of her planted corn, Ada grunted as she tried to move a barrel. It barely budged. "Damn it." She ran the back of her forearm over her forehead.

"Need some help? Cass asked.

Ada turned around. "No, fuck it. It can stay where it is. I was hoping to fit one more barrel in here. But three will be enough for now."

Cass took a step toward her and backed up immediately. "Good lord, what is that smell? Is that the concoction?"

"This is early stages. Fermenting. Won't be done for a few weeks."

"It stinks."

"It works," said Ada. "Come to the other shed and help me with the bottles. Still have a couple people that have to stop by and grab theirs."

"Sure thing." Cass walked with her. "So, I take it Lena went out with a search party?"

Ada stopped walking. "No, why would you say that?"

"Walt gave her that green mini-van to ride around in so she didn't have to walk or bother you for a ride to and from town."

"Okay."

"It's gone."

"I didn't even notice. I..." Ada switched directions. Instead of going to the other shed, she hightailed it to the house, barreling in the back door.

Trixie peeped a shriek. "You scared me. I was making you breakfast."

"Where's Lena?" Ada asked.

"Still sleeping, I guess. I saw her last night. She went to bed early." Trixie's eyes widened. "What's wrong?"

The back door opened again and Cass ran in. "Oh my God, you run fast for an old lady. Is she here?"

"Sleeping," said Trixie. "But Ada is worrying me."

Ada was worried too. Something didn't sit right with her and immediately she walked out of the kitchen to the stairs and up.

Cass followed. "Ada, maybe she joined a team and didn't want to tell you."

Ada didn't reply. She got to the top of the stairs and walked to Lena's room. She brought her hand to the door and it opened when she knocked.

The room was empty and the bed was made.

"See," Cass said. "She went on the search party."

On the bed was a folded piece of paper and Ada lifted it. After unfolding it, her eyes skimmed it. "No, Cass, she didn't." She handed the note to Cass. A note that simply read, 'Ada, thanks for everything. I went home.'

Los Angeles, CA

She was able to make it within a mile of her home, then Lena had to stop, the roads were just not passible. Some of the freeway was covered and it made for a bumpy ride, then there was too much of the fungus to even attempt to drive.

The fungus reminded her of old tree roots, long, wayward, and thick. It spread about like veins across the roads, wrapping up the sides of buildings, all covered in this thick multi-shade of green grassy-looking substance.

The perfectly maintained lawns of her neighborhood were still lush and green, untouched by the fungus growth. The driveways and pillars weren't so lucky. The corners and roofs of homes seemed to be prime growth spots.

Art and Niles had talked about how it would destroy everything that wasn't alive—she finally understood what they meant when she saw some of the homes. It had only been days, yet the brick exteriors of some appeared to be crumbling, as if the fungus was squeezing it apart.

The walk to her own home was a painful one. Each step breaking her heart knowing what she would find. Trixie told her that her family had passed because of the original event, the pred bug spray that took out most of the world. With the heat, she knew what she could physically face.

It wasn't so much that she had to touch and see her family, she just needed to be where they were.

It had been days, and the usually temperate weather of Los Angeles was hot and muggy.

Lena approached her driveway. The gate was open and, like the pillars, covered with the fungus. The driveway was slick, and it felt like she was walking in a creek, thick stones beneath her feet making an unstable ground.

Her grass was untouched, as were her imported bushes and rose garden.

The fungus covered her double doors and the brick of her home. She knew the door would be impossible to open, so she walked around to the back.

The fungus made no sense to her. It looked as if it attacked with no rhyme or reason. Wanting to become one with nature, leaving everything that God created alone.

The entire pool area was covered, the statues tightly wound up with the growth, yet the water in the pool was untouched.

The fungus hadn't fully reached the sliding glass door of the kitchen, just part of the base and Lena slid it open enough to squeeze through.

The home had a weird sour and musky smell. She entered into the breakfast area, just near the kitchen. While the growth had crept into the breakfast nook, the kitchen was untouched. Her shiny appliances still glimmered as if just cleaned.

Trixie told her that her family had all passed away in the family room. Both children on the sofa, her mother on the love seat and John in a chair.

Knowing that was where she had to go, Lena headed that way.

With each step not only was it emotionally difficult, it was increasingly physically difficult as well. It was like a forest with unbreakable limbs, a prison of nature, and Lena squeezed through each opening she could, climbing her way into the family room.

She made it to the doorway and couldn't go any farther. The entire room was filled. The branch-style fungus broke through the walls and created a gate in the doorway she could not pass.

She looked through. The sun peeked through the windows and gave enough light for her to see the outline of the sofa and loveseat. The green mounds of what looked like clovers and moss were on the furniture and Lena knew what that was.

It was her family.

She began to sob. Looping her fingers through the moss vines, holding on and staring out like a prisoner from her cell.

Lena was a prisoner of her own nightmare.

She wasn't going anywhere, not yet. There she'd stand looking at what remained, praying they hadn't suffered and missing them more than her soul could bear.

She didn't know how long she would stay or even if she would go at all. She'd made it home, to her family, and at that moment, that was all that mattered to Lena.

24.
DOME

The police station looked like a war room. Maps covered the wall, the white board had numerous notes, and pictures printed from cell phone footage were plastered on the wall. Mark stood before a crowded room, trying to engage and answer while everyone seemed to talk at once.

Cass was engrossed looking at the pictures.

"This thing," Mark said, "spreads over a hundred feet an hour. That's a mile a day."

"Anything on the other side of Miller Run Road," someone said, "will bring it to Griffin in less than three days."

"No. No," Art said strong. "All of you are wrong. It's not the *Blob*, it doesn't move like a river or like lava. It's like a pebble in a pond. It spreads that way. Wherever it was dropped. If anyone or anything was dead from OG-22X, then there were flies, if there were flies, they carried it."

"Then it's here," Mark said, his words bringing immediate silence to the room. "It's here in Griffin. We've had seven deaths from it. Why haven't I seen it?"

229

Niles answered, "Because the bodies are in Fillman's freezers. The temperature is slowing the growth, but trust me, if we go look I'll bet it's there. Just waiting for its chance to escape."

"Jesus Christ," Mark said. "What do we do?"

"Burn Fillman's," Art suggested.

"Don't be ridiculous," said Eb. "Cremate the bodies and douse the place with Ada's concoction. We know it works and kills it immediately. In fact, we need to all be armed and ready with the stuff. Hit it as soon as we see it. Because I don't see how we're gonna be spared."

Mark faced Art. "So will it hit us like the other towns? I mean, you said it wasn't moving like lava, but will it spread here?"

"Eventually," Art said, "yes."

An eruption of moans filled the room.

Then Ada spoke loudly and with a firm voice. "What is our objective here? We're losing focus. Mark sent everyone out to scout and fact find. Well, you got it. It's out there. We know we can't worry about it popping up here and there in town. We can squash them little fires when they happen. We need to treat this fungus like a wildfire burning outside our town and we have to stop it from reaching us. We can't save the world, and I'm pretty positive we aren't the only ones left, but we can save our town. We just need to think grand scale."

"Niles and I, if we have time," Art said, "could possibly create a bacterium that can kill this fungus."

"Um…no," Ada said. "You boys created enough of a mess."

"What do you suggest, Miss Frontierswoman?" Art asked.

"Beat and treat like the thing it is…fungus. We aren't talking about a skin thing," Ada said. "This is a soil fungus, whether it's a million years old or not. There are certain paths it will not cross. You yourself said it won't touch nature, it doesn't cross water. We create a barrier around town. A mile out all the way around. We overturn soil, we plant, we make a barrier of life around us it won't cross."

Art laughed. "Do you know how long that will take? Maybe a year. It will be upon us by then."

"We hold it at bay," Ada said.

"How?" Art asked.

"We spray. We see it closing in," Ada said. "We spray to kill it using my stuff."

"How do you propose we do that?" asked Art.

Kit spoke up. "We have a pilot lying in bed three at the bingo clinic, I'm pretty sure he can fly a crop duster."

"It's a good plan," Niles said. "But the barrier you create will have to be wide, I'm talking whatever you plant has to have a safety measure."

"Things die," Mark added. "We'll have to plan for that. And the areas where we can't plant or build a moat. What about those, what do we do for those areas?"

Cass turned from the wall of pictures and joined the conversation. "Glass."

Everyone looked at her.

"Has anyone looked at these pictures?" Cass asked. "Do you see the common denominator here? Where the fungus isn't? The windows."

"Cass, sweetheart." Mark chuckled. "As great of an idea as that is, we can't build a dome around Griffin."

"Don't talk down to me," Cass said. "Glass has to be the solution."

"It's inorganic." Art walked to the pictures. "Glass is inorganic. Cass you're brilliant. Mold can grow on it, but it's highly unlikely fungus can settle. It can try but it won't attach long enough to release the properties to break down. And glass is not the only inorganic substance. There are many others we can use. In fact this…is our solution." Art tapped the pictures. "This backing up Ada's nature barrier may be what saves this town."

"I am all for saving this town," Mark said. "But you are saying building a glass wall around the circumference of our town is our only chance."

Art shook his head. "No, the fungus could die off if it has nothing else to grab on to. That's possible. Not probable. I'm saying, as insane as it sounds, as incredibly hard as it will be to pull off, you, Mr. Mayor, have been given the solution. Now it's up to you and everyone in this town," Art said. "What are you going to do?"

25.
EVERMORE

November 20

Griffin, AZ

It was the last one.

The steady but fading sound of the crop-dusting plane made Cass sad. She knew it would be the last one she would hear. Ada just didn't have the supplies to make a huge drop. What she did have and was fermenting was for spot killing when the fungus popped up in Griffin. Over the previous six months it had shown growth, maybe on a rooftop or parking lot. Nothing major and nothing they weren't able to stop.

At first it was like waiting for the predicted storm that didn't come, the fungus was growing in areas around them, thickening and covering, but keeping its distance. It allowed those not working on the barrier to go out and scavenge whatever they could get.

Fifty-four more people made their way into town. Walking there, climbing through the new world of nature, bringing with them very few belongings. They all became part of the Griffin family.

One person never did return…Lena.

Ada and Cass waited for her, but she never came back. Cass understood Lena's decision, but wondered if she had tried to return but couldn't. Was she out there somewhere trying to survive? Was there a chance she'd eventually make her way back to Griffin?

The one thing Cass refused to believe was that Lena had died.

Too many had left the earth senselessly. Lena's survival was something she held onto.

In fact, in the beginning there was a lot of hope. Cass had hope, like many others that maybe the fungus would stop, that Griffin and the area close by would be spared. But that didn't happen.

Once Seaver was consumed, it wasn't long before they had to bring out the crop duster. Nolan, the pilot, did a great job. Usually the dusting would stop the growth for a week or so, then he had to go back out.

Cass wished that they'd be able to continue dusting, at least until the natural barrier was finished. But it didn't work out that way and that frightened her. A few sections of glass had been erected. It didn't need to be too tall, just high enough. The natural barrier was close to seventy percent complete. At least the first round. They'd go back and add that safety measure if they could.

It was a lot of ground to cover and a part of Griffin was still so vulnerable. That section, west of town, right where the welcome arch was located, was open.

It was also the place Cass went to every single day.

It wasn't long before that day when she could gaze outward and just see road.

Now she looked out and all she saw was a wall of the growing fungus in the distance.

It was still far away, and it hadn't moved in weeks. But it was tall, like a forest; the fungus not only spread wide, in some areas it grew upwards, taller than the tallest tree she had ever seen.

It moved too fast for there to be any positive outcome when it was all said and done.

She spent a lot of time thinking of those astronauts on the Space Station. How the world looked to them. Could they see Griffin, a bare spot in an encapsulated world of new growth?

After visiting Ada, she parked her car by Eb's shop and walked through town, a loaf of homemade bread in one hand and bottle of wine in the other. She passed Brass Balls and Beers and could hear the music inside, but it wasn't coming from a juke box. The power had gone out months earlier. It was a group of musicians playing. The laughter and noise carried out into the street. She was envious of those in town who lived life to the fullest and didn't think about what was to come.

Every time she did that, she remembered they were literally on borrowed time. She hated when those thoughts hit her.

She stopped at the end of town, just at the arch, staring out.

Was the fungus still at a distance, did it move closer?

"I thought I'd find you here," Kit said, coming from behind.

"Oh, hey, I'm sorry. Yeah. I wanted to do my daily check."

"And?"

"Does it look closer to you?" Cass asked.

"No. And it isn't. I went out this morning."

Cass nodded.

"Cass, we'll burn it if we need to. It hasn't moved."

"It doesn't mean it won't."

"You're being this way because of the crop dusting."

"Yeah, our safety net is gone."

"Don't think that way. We're still here. Art said there is a chance it could die off. Hold onto that. And for today, can you just pretend all is fine?"

235

Cass finally turned and faced him. "I'll try. I mean everyone else in this town is."

"No, they aren't pretending. They really are grateful," Kit said then looked down to the items she held in her hands. "Are they for us?"

"Oh. Shit. Yes. Ada made bread and sent wine." She handed them to Kit. "How's the turkey?"

"Considering it's the first one I made on a wood burning stove, I think it's almost done. The whole house smells like Thanksgiving."

"Well it is."

"You bagged a great turkey," Kit said.

"I bagged twelve." Cass laughed. "People need to start eating the game around here before the game start eating everything else. I'm killing more meat than they can eat."

"Did you ever wonder about that?" Kit asked. "I mean the world is supposed to be dead, right? Where's all the game coming from?"

Cass didn't say anything.

"I know you look out every day and all you see is death creeping our way. But there's life out there. It's Thanksgiving, Cass, let's be thankful we're still here, because we very well could not have been."

"You're right."

"I know I'm right," Kit said. "I also know my little pep talk here will last only until tomorrow. So…let's go home."

He wouldn't get an argument from her, she never stayed long at that spot. Just a brief daily stop, a reminder that no matter how bright and cheerful life seemed to be, out there somewhere, was something waiting to take it away.

As she walked down the street with Kit, she glanced over her shoulder once more to what loomed on the horizon.

That moment was so indicative of her life and how she had lived it for the last eight years.

Moving forward, yet always looking back to the dark behind her. Only this time it was different; she didn't just choose to survive, she and everyone else in Griffin fought to survive.

Cass had to keep reminding herself of that. She had to try to find the optimist when the realist in her tried to surface.

No matter how many times she looked back to the bad, waiting for it to swoop in and snatch it all away, she had to focus on what was before her, what she lived for, what she and the others had. Whether it was short term or for the long haul, bottom line was…Griffin had beaten the odds. The world had been swallowed by an insurmountable force, but not Griffin. Griffin lived and thrived. And as much as she fought to admit it, Cass, like those in the town of Griffin, embraced her second chance at life.

ABOUT THE AUTHOR

Jacqueline Druga is a native of Pittsburgh, PA. Her works include genres of all types but she favors post-apocalypse and apocalypse writing.

For updates on new releases you can find the author on:

Facebook: @jacquelinedruga

Twitter: @gojake

www.jacquelinedruga.com

What we Become by Jacqueline Druga

Like many, Mackenzie Garret complains about the weather. It is the hottest summer anyone can remember. The high temperatures are out of control with no end in sight. Until it all changes.

Overnight, blue skies become gray, and the hot, humid weather turns to rain, then snow, then ice as the temperature plummets.

The entire northern half of the country is thrown into chaos as blow by blow, storm after storm, nature rips into the world, tearing it apart. Towns and cities are evacuated, and Mac and her family are forced to leave their world behind and face a treacherous journey south to safety.

Will they make it, or will they be left behind in this new, frozen world?

ACKNOWLEDGEMENTS

Huge thank you to Dark Heart Designs for the wonderful cover and to AI Jones for all your help.

www.ingramcontent.com/pod-product-compliance
Lightning Source LLC
Chambersburg PA
CBHW031721170626
46808CB00005B/1832